Books by LARRY WOIWODE

NOVELS

What I'm Going to Do, I Think (1 9 6 9)
Beyond the Bedroom Wall (1 9 7 5)
Poppa John (1 9 8 1)

POEMS

Even Tide (1 9 7 7)

Poppa John

Poppa John

LARRY
WOIWODE

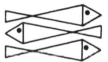

Farrar, Straus and Giroux

NEW YORK

Copyright © *1981* by *Larry Woiwode*
All rights reserved
Library of Congress catalog card number: 81–12590
Published simultaneously in Canada by
McGraw-Hill Ryerson Ltd., Toronto
Printed in the United States of America
Designed by Guy Fleming
First edition, 1981
ISBN 0-374-52673-7 (pbk)

for CAROLE

those Willow years

HE is at once sculptor and sculpture; he is a man at the farthest borderline between reality and dream, and he stands with both feet in both realms. The actor's power of self-suggestion is so great that he can bring about in his body not only inner and psychological but even outer and physical changes. And when one ponders on the miracle of Konnersreuth, whereby a simple peasant girl experiences every Friday the passion of Christ, with so strong an imaginative power that her hands and feet show wounds and she actually weeps tears of blood, one may judge to what wonders and to what a mysterious world the art of acting may lead; for it is assuredly by the same process that the player, in Shakespeare's words, changes utterly his accustomed visage, his aspect and carriage, his whole being, and can weep for Hecuba and make others weep. Every night the actor bears the stigmata, which his imagination inflicts upon him, and bleeds from a thousand wounds.

— MAX REINHARDT,

in "The Actor,"

Encyclopaedia Britannica,

1949 edition

FRIDAY /

December 23

I

"Love?"

Her back was to him, from the sound of her voice, as his was to her.

Love? He turned in the bluish shadow at the back corner of their apartment, away from the ornate sideboard that they used to keep stocked as a bar, and saw her, indeed, facing away, under the arch between the dining and living rooms, in the direction of the morning light. The silver cast of it entering the windows at this hour was concentrated at her outlines and pressed her figure, one hand up over a shoulder, into his senses. He went toward her and in a trick of the brilliance against her had to stop so suddenly he tilted and leaned over her in a way that registered in him as *tent pole*.

He suffered a flash of a picture of such a pole, with the tent draped beyond and swaying in a faint wind: smoky light in its folds.

Her pearl-and-black dress, undone to the waist, bared a fulcrum of her scented skin, where thread-like vessels of red and violet were scattered in irregular wriggles. The ribbony straps of one of those see-through brassieres that she'd begun to wear (woman's perennial yoke, which some—or actresses, anyway—were beginning to discard) framed her upper spine and the tapering mane of down over its ridges, tempting his mouth.

Ah, he'd been staring into his face in the mirror at the back of the sideboard—this much came—trying to recapture the fragments of his waking dream, which had jarred him out of an hour's sleep, and which kept telescoping into him faster than his logic-tainted senses could travel, and then— He shook his head. And now lay, it felt, in a shambles over the sideboard.

And where had tent pole come from?

"Will you do it, love?"

In what sense? he nearly asked.

Twelve years as Poppa John. Twelve years and now this dead end in which Poppa John wasn't to exist. Yet Poppa John's boundaries, like old grave wrappings, clung to him, informing every footstep. Over the months that he'd been home since his "death," it was as if the two of them had resumed their first year of marriage, though both were closing out their sixties; our senile honeymoon, he'd said more than once, trying to deflect her interest from his real concern. For he felt that a gun was at his ear, thrusting into their lovemaking the heightened charge that possible death hurries in on heaving

4

wings, and the act itself was his only means of tripping its explosive eruptions while remaining intact.

His long, bent-back, spatulate fingers, which
he hated, twitched at her lowest button, as though
now he couldn't decide whether to close or un-
sheath her, and he wondered whether the competi-
tive people who designed such clothes always
assumed a husband would be handy to help, or if,
in their high-mindedness, they could care.

She turned to him.

Her lips were parted and, free of their usual
makeup, looked fuller, more of a piece with her.
Color clouded her face, as her eyes wavered in and
out of focus.

"You're not really sure, then," she said.

"But I am."

"You were so positive when you first mentioned
it."

"The sight of you like this has interrupted the,
ah— I have to train my thoughts toward that
singular course."

Her eyes swayed and probed as if to make
their way through the verbal foliage of this, and
then went aside, unfulfilled, in a gray-blue swerve.
She turned again. "Let's just go," she said. "Do me."

He buttoned her up and she stepped in silence,
still in her stockings, across the parquet and into the
powder room that they'd persuaded their landlord
to let them add to the vestibule this year, after

Poppa John

Poppa John had started spending his days at home. "You want it *here?*" the landlord had asked, staring at the chalk lines they'd drawn over the floor as if they were saw cuts. "Well, if it's going to bring up the value of this place, and not flood the gent below, you know, go ahead, I guess." He pulled at a mustache he'd begun to affect in the spring, an overweight (but dieting) bachelor in his fifties, just coming onto the knowledge, considering his newly raffish appearance, that physical life was finite. "But it's a good thing you asked. I'd break your lease as soon as look at you, if you didn't. I mean, I love you folks, but the rent you're paying is ridiculous for here." And then, half out the door: "You can't rip out any cabinets or fixtures if you move, you know. I couldn't stand for that. I'd get my lawyer." The clong of the door. Gone.

And Poppa John had thought, The cost, the cost, and then: *Lay not up for yourselves treasures upon earth, where moth and rust doth corrupt, and where thieves break through and steal, but . . .*

He went to the phone and plugged it into the recording machine and made sure the tape was set. Why wasn't that young agent ever making a call? His keys. He'd had them, sometime before he stood sightless at the sideboard, he was sure of that. He went into their bedroom, rubbing and patting over his pockets and vest with a new nervousness to those fingers he preferred not to look at, and saw a

6

tilting replication of his height, from shoulders to thighs, like an opening book, in the mirror of the oak bureau, but no keys on its top.

He stepped into the bathroom, which he had to make sure he used, now, every time before he went out, due to the effect of nerves on his age, and there they were, raying out from their ring like a sunburst, on the edge of the still-full tub. The clothes that he'd shed before he'd bathed lay around as if a second-story man had got into the room in the time since and scattered them in malicious senselessness.

Suddenly he had the hiccups.

"What is it, Poppa John?"

Her face, caught from behind in a knit cloche that held her heavy hair in a blue skein, seemed to float up at him, detached and fragilely luminous against the wall of brick. A cab came by with its horn held down, echoing everywhere, and he swung toward it with such suddenness he nearly collided with the press of people navigating Forty-second at noon.

"Easy, gramps," somebody said.

An oval poster of a Christmas decoration, with tinsel encircling it, hung from a lamppost standard above, which was also twined with tinsel, and beyond that, in jolting focus, a rumbling chain of cars and cabs crossed the arcadelike bridge above Park, their colors flashing past its posts and metal

7

scrollwork like a conflagration. And beyond all that, Grand Central: with its brown and ominous façade, breaking into figures and wings at the top, in the precious space of air preserved above it. Then the sidewalk underfoot trembled and shook with the ironbound bulk of another subway coming in.

She took his lapel and drew him next to the building, beside her, as if out of rain, and an enveloping thought that had felt as weighty and substantial as the approaching train, just before she spoke, was up into the air again, gone.

"I'm worried about you, Poppa John. No, now listen. You've been entirely unlike yourself since we started getting ready to leave. Now, shall we go through with this, or does it suddenly seem wrong to you?"

There was a ratlike frieze in the rock molding at his temple that made his left eye ache. He passed a hand over his stubbly beard and squinted the eye, nearly achieving his famous wink, and then batted his eyelashes at her from out of his most charming-seductive face.

"To tell the truth, dear, I'm toplessly excited," he said, trying to sound like Poppa John, now that they were in public, but was startled (as she was, from the width of her eyes in their studying clarity concentrated by the cold) at his modifier, which seemed to have flown into his head from a bar across town. One of her curled, mascaraed lashes had striped her eye shadow, he saw, which gave her a clownish, childlike look, and he was treading within the delicate confusion of whether to point this out.

"I meant, I haven't really felt like it's Christmas. That is, I haven't felt the anticipatory flutter that usually comes a week or two ahead for me and accompanies the, ah . . . I haven't felt anything, until we decided to do this, and then all of these people—" He indicated with his hand, and it was shouldered back. "Well, *some* of these people have reinforced my sense of— Whit tea! it's hard to talk here! Do you have the bankbook?"

"Do your knees hurt?"

"Is that non sequitur, or what?"

"You've been complaining about them lately. The walking. You complained of them Sunday."

"I did?" His eyes went from one face to another in the crowd as if there were someone there to explain this. "Aren't we there?"

"Yes, we're outside the bank." She drew her fur coat closer around her throat.

"Doesn't seem right to me."

"What do you mean?"

"Or did I pocket that thing?"

He started slamming his hands over his topcoat and saw that he'd forgotten his gloves. He made twiddling motions in front of her face with those hateful fingers. " 'Tis nipping and shrewd, this air, Celia, sweets, and eager, too, like yours truly, ah-gah!"

Her ready laughter rose from the interior he'd

traveled for thirty years and he felt, in the space of
relief that came, the lost and weighty thought draw
close again, hovering. Then her purse popped open
under his eyes, metaled jaws, releasing areas of her
and their apartment into the atmosphere, and, as if on
those fumes, the blood-brown book in its plastic
case came up. But, as he went to take it, she gripped
hard: white kid gloves.

"Is it wise to be doing this, Poppa John, at this
particular time?"

"Perfectly so. I'll be at work next week."

"Why don't you go ahead back to the apartment and let me pick up some things on my own.
Essentials."

"But we decided. We—" There was a line of
reasoning here he couldn't put into proper sequence.

"If you're worried about the money, I'll gladly
wait for another time. We can celebrate in January.
Or March."

"Oh, no, no. That's not the worry, if there is
one. Who ever heard of Christmas in March! Come
on."

He took off in the stride he used making rounds
and felt her grip at his coat sleeve. He slowed to her
stately walk, guiding her through the crowd with a
steadiness provided at least partly by her touch, and
then ushered her into the revolving door, and stepped
into the section behind. The whorl of air compressed
his eardrums as he pushed, while scattered lights and

reflections went flying aside at eye level, above other entering heads, and then in the warm wash of the bank he stopped, astonished.

He thought he'd heard pealing bells echoing across the interior of the gray-stone building, which was as spacious as St. Pat's, with a fifty-foot arch of bluish windows fanning across its opposite end. The magnificent ceiling, yet above this arch, was beamed and coffered with hardwood in ever-decreasing geo-metrics, the coffers painted or covered over inside in tile-like patterns that appeared Moorish. The sound of bells seemed to be projecting through these decorations down over him in a clangorous din, and the coffers glowed with an illumination he'd never noticed before, as if the ceiling were a grid leading upward into further intricacies of design to trans-parency.

"Happy holidays to you and the missus!" a cheery voice called, and he turned and had to grapple with what he was seeing to make it register.

Just inside the door, a man in a tuxedo sat up on a dais, with an aluminum Christmas tree beside him, at a console, an electric organ, rendering a source to the amplified noise of "Joy to the World!" and now the man was nodding and smiling, as if he knew he'd surprised Poppa John, and was amused at this. He called, "Happy holidays to you and the missus, sir! May the season hold all that you've hoped for!" And then tossed his fluffy hair around as he thundered down on a series of chords and brought the carillon in again on the chorus.

A current of embarrassment covered Poppa John; yet he felt cradled, in a deeper throe, attuned to the tones permeating him, and participating in them, until his genitals began to thicken with an anticipatory swell. This gun-gorged honeymoon. He started for the end of the bank, toward the teller's window with the initial of his last name above it, feeling the tug again at his coat sleeve, and this time, being pulled in so many directions, nearly lost his footing on the stone floor. And saw that he was wearing his ragged tennis sneakers. In this weather? With his three-piece suit and best topcoat? Was it that bad? Is that why she'd asked about his knees?

"Goodness, Poppa John," she whispered. "It's obvious you're not used to me along. You're *stalking* everywhere today." She drew him closer. "Don't you think that's clever?"

"What?"

"The fellow playing carols."

"It's a dream."

He went to a marble-topped table against the wall—one of several set between columns of different kinds of marble that lined the place—and took out his bankbook. A noise like the lobby of Grand Central. Cut through by the carol, whose continuing circulation of melody in his nerves and flesh, and reverberations from the slab where his forearms lay and from the stone around, squeezed up a tear like alkaline gall into one eye, then the other. Why did these simple words and songs affect him so much, as they did, every year, as if they'd never existed, and had sprung fresh from his imagination? Joy to the world, indeed.

He shook his head, and the three brass lamps along the table, like desk lamps, with oblong burnished shades, and with tricky designs and mosaics on them (which he looked at now as if newly minted; a lamb, a star? a dragon?), firmed into brightness, and then he saw with a shock that the brass legs that supported the table were, at their bottoms, after a swirl of figures, hooves.

She sat on a stone bench beside him, glancing around, and then turned and whispered up at him, as if indeed they were in church, "How much do you think?"

A diminutive uniformed guard who looked older than Poppa John, white-haired and wizened, with a pistol on a harness at his hip, came up, feebly humming the carol, and put some deposit and withdrawal slips into the glass rack at the back of the table. There was an obsidian plaque there, with a hole bored down its center (a perfect place for a person with hooves like those below to sharpen his tail, Poppa John thought) where a ball-point usually stood, chained, now a vacancy in black; the guard ran a finger over it, and murmured, "Robber," and then went off, humming, to the next table. He'd inserted a card in the rack that read: *We will remain open this evening until 8:00 PM.*

Poppa John felt frisked, livid. "How much will you need?" he asked, and yanked out a withdrawal slip.

"I estimate about a hundred and fifty dollars, but I could easily manage with less."

The amount registered with an impact he tried to set his face against. He took out his pen and glasses and peered at the balance: eight hundred and some. A formerly untouchable account, down from five figures to this, because of that damned powder room. Besides being accustomed to an income of a hundred thousand a year, some years more. They would have to have two hundred dollars for the January rent, if they didn't want to trip their newly tensed landlord toward eviction, the hundred and fifty she wanted (what on earth did she plan to get with that?), plus money for him to shop. He wrote his legal name on the slip and then fiddled over it with the pen, deciding that for now he'd withdraw four hundred, and that any more would be overstepping their limits, as if this weren't—he really wasn't sure of work yet—but saw his hand write, instead, in shakily pinched movements that became autonomous, *seven.*

So as not to seem cheap to her? There were bursts of perspiration under his beret. Robber. He'd watched the money she'd been putting aside for years in her jewelry box, and which he'd surreptitiously started stealing from, dwindle away for groceries over the past weeks. His fingers twitched and curled farther back from the pen at the figure, but then the cash, he thought, nearly saying it aloud as he stuck away his glasses, was as safe in their pockets as in the bank.

She was standing beside him. "That much?" she asked.

"It's all right. I smell promise." Provoked by her perfume? Every external caught at him. He covered the balance, which she must know, and turned to the window behind him. Was that light beaming out from the cage of brassy bars? A camera stood there on a metal pole. There were two ahead in line, and he wasn't sure he could bear the wait, stiff and fevered with anxiety, which blanked him, and then he was next.

He placed the slip in the bankbook, placed the book down on the tray in front of the bars, placed his hands there and straightened—all with the studied precision of being on camera so often, nearly every day, that his smallest gesture was measured against an outer eye. "Two hundred in a money order," he said. His business voice was giving; his lips shook.

The teller, who had turned away, with his back to him, was checking in a file, as if he didn't believe the balance, or had to laugh at it, or doubted Poppa

John's identity, with that shaky signature, and the
thought of having to wait another second sent up
an urge to grab at the bars in front of him and—
    This came with such truncated violence no con-
clusion appeared. The teller worked a check
machine and counted cash and then slipped an envelope with a wreath of holly printed on it onto
the marble tray, and said, "God bless you."
    Poppa John turned away and then turned back,
stunned; how was he to respond to that? He was
staring at a youngish man whose brown eyes and
elegant hair reminded him, in a tug at credulity, of
his agent. Was this merely business, or the fellow's
contribution to the season? Now Poppa John had to
respond himself, after this space of staring, or else—
Then a voice behind him said, "Pardon me, sir, if
you're through."
    There were a dozen now waiting.
    He took Celia over to the wall, next to a black-
and-green column that turned blue, from shadow or
the false color his confusion could spread over surfaces, and handed her two hundred in cash. He
clapped the rest of what remained in the envelope
into his wallet.
    "Goodness," she said. "This is more than I
asked for. Well, all right"—she put it away—"where
shall we meet?"
    "In a restaurant close. Or right back here. In
the bank here."

"Which?"

He'd lunched in a score of places in the vicinity, but none came to mind in the haze around the area his attention kept reverting to, where the essential missing thought had left a vacancy. "I don't care. Name one."

"You know this neighborhood better than I do. There must be some quiet place you particularly like."

"Any. I don't care." He was angry now. If the thought could be recovered, then the day might begin as it should. "Oh, hell, this is such a bother. And they'll all be packed today, anyway. Let's just meet at home."

"If that's what you want."

"I said it," he said, and went at his usual pace, ahead of her, across the building and into the revolving door.

He'd stepped into the same quadrant as a model, from her clothes and makeup, who glanced back at him in fury while he tried to manage a mincing step that would keep him from constantly bumping into her back, or walking down her shoes, and outside, as he hurried into an apology, she looked him up and down, and said, "Is this how you old jokers get your kicks?"

She was off in clacking strides and again Celia had his arm.

"*Really*, Poppa John," she said, and laughed

bursts of frost into the air. "You must have startled her. Please, won't you come with me?"

"Then how could I shop for you?" he said. This was a portion of the line of logic he'd been looking for earlier, outside here, and now the cold helped it form: his original idea had been that no matter how broke they were, with no prospects of money in sight, it shouldn't spoil their Christmas, as in O. Henry; indeed, they should go and get the gifts they'd been meaning to get for one another for the last several years and never had, for whatever reasons, trusting that the additional money would arrive when it was needed, partly by putting pressure on the need. This last he hadn't mentioned, and was aware of the pseudo-Christian fatuity it implied (though it was a ploy many Christians fell prey to), when Scriptures actually said that they were to provide things honest in the sight of *all men*, not just God, rather than try to tempt God, like sacrificing pagans, to perform. And now, from this series of turns, he was provided with the leverage he'd been looking for; his smile came clear.

"I'm going east, my dear, as in the Scots highroad," he said. "You go west."

He took off in his walk.

Now the cold came over his back below his shoulders, as though studying him there, and he was grateful for his vest. Had somebody acknowledged him? Farther along, he heard a whisper of "Poppa John" and performed the wave that had become his trademark—his open hand up beside his face with the wink, and then rolling slowly right while his smile widened, in his modification of the old black-bottom 23 skiddoo, and then the clack of his teeth at the end as he closed it off, with a flourish like a conductor's. Then the expectant look of interest, in which you could read his willingness to listen to whatever you had to say, regardless of its implications, without the prison of judgment confining you. He was a listener. He was a confessor, in a sense, and a savant. A man contented in his years and the wisdom they'd brought, and willing to share that, according to audience standards.

And he (he himself, that is) preferred this broad anonymity of the street, where you could imagine yourself to be whatever the faces or the shifting prism of influences called up, to the private solitary sort of closeted retreat, where you were caught within the inescapable sack of the self that you'd been in since birth.

Who or what indeed could free you from this body that bore your death?

For a dozen years he'd been Poppa John to millions of viewers, of every age and sort, and more of them had watched his death this fall, it was estimated, than the funeral of young President Kennedy, several seasons ago. As the final stages of it went winding down over a week of late-afternoon

19

segments, bars became packed and crowds gathered at storefront windows where televisions were playing (while in some parochial schools sets were brought into the assembly halls, he'd heard, so beloved was he, still, of the nuns—an aura always about you, once you'd learned to apply their standards to yourself): cars were parked wherever space could be found, or were double-parked, and, in a few cases, abandoned, with traffic and crowd problems reported in the city and across the states on the final day, as he signed off his life with one last faint suggestion of the wave.

Celia went out immediately afterward, to be alone, she said, and found their whole neighborhood silent.

He turned north on Lexington, whose browns and grays were overlaid with garish signs that gave it the appearance of a pinched and hustling Park, and saw, in the lane of sky opening ahead over him, that it might snow.

The viewer estimate was by one of the established rating firms. Mention of it was made in *TV Guide*, in a follow-up to the cover feature they'd done on him a few issues before the end. They'd come to him with apologies about a superficial and ironic piece they'd printed on him early in his tenure, blaming the tastes of a previous editor, and asked him to give them a chance to make up for that. Silver innuendos. He'd let his agent handle it all; overtures of the sort left him unmoved, and he'd come to mistrust any pandering to his position as Poppa John. But he felt it was time to let Celia see the light.

She'd encouraged him to try out for a peripheral character on one of those soaps that supposedly depict American family life and its disruptions, and he'd gone ahead, partly because he was between jobs and saw it as a possible well-paying lark, and he'd stepped into the part as into a pair of pants on the way to the door, that quick. "Poppa John," as he came into being that day, was based on particulars of his preacher grandfather, plus an early turn at Stratford in the *Henrys* as Sir John Falstaff, whose earthy configurations were still plumbable to round matters out when he read for the role; and Poppa John developed with such scope and naturalness, there were letters every week, bags of them, from people he'd never met, addressing him as a family member or an intimate. The producers took note of this, and in a while nearly every other segment revolved in some way around him. They loaned him a secretary to help with his correspondence. They were nice, then.

Celia said he'd found his natural field, though the environment wasn't what one would wish upon an actor who'd begun with a serious intent, and claimed he was elevated above his surroundings "like a ship on the Hudson stew. There's a quality you have that makes you as real there"—she pointed at the television—"behind glass, as when you're beside me like this. You're a double being."

Then last year a battle of ratings between the two networks, or the two that counted, began, with audience interest shifting to a program whose emphasis was sliding from the family base to a looser love life among the young, and he became, for the staff and the network he was loyal to, the sacrifice.

Rumors of his illness began to circulate among minor characters on the show, and the eventual outcome became such a well-guarded secret that even the faithful regulars, who'd worked with him for years, were never fully let in on it, in case the tactics should have to be reversed. None of his scenes for the final two months were taped. He did them live. That trusted and competent. And a surer image, also, for the end.

He was first hospitalized nine months ago, and immediately the ratings went up. He brazened out his usual self as much as he was able, being bedridden, for about a month, while a team of doctors—new actors, new young nurses around, the hospital interest—and then consultants to the doctors were called in, and all shook their heads over him. And then this group, with other attachments, moved into the orbit that it was said the audience was now interested in.

An elderly black cleaning lady, who entered his hospital room every day with a pail and mop, became his Mistress Quickly. He called her sweet woman (slurring and opening "woman" out as wide toward "mama" as he could) rather than sweet wench, and some college professors wrote in to say that they saw the parallels with *Henry IV, Part Two.* What did those people do with their days? One afternoon, as he lay in his bed, the sweet woman uncovered his feet and began to rub them as if he were Ivan Ilyich, because once writers are on to something, there's no sparing other writers, and no time for thought of overlaps or anachronistic mixings. If they could have worked in Huckleberry Finn, they would have. They'd never leaped in such happy unison through so many hoops.

He transformed the black woman, as she rubbed and talked in a gruff manner that wasn't intended to fool anybody, into Celia. Only Celia would know how to minister to him like this. Only Celia loved the conformation of his feet as much as he loved having feet to walk on and have rubbed, and she knew what regions of his body and brain the nerve ends in every area of them reached into.

Then he was out of the hospital, and back in the book-lined study that he'd retired from his insurance business into, but restricted in his movements, so that the writing of the show, of necessity, now, had to center even more around him. At least once a week he was given a lengthy speech that was well written in the manner that laymen call inspired, and so elegiac that only an actor of his experience could skirt the shame of sentiment. He fed the writers material of his own, and one day told the story of his grandfather building a wagon for an orphan, revealing at the end, in a loop of evasiveness and diffidence he snapped tight, that he was the orphan.

And then back to the hospital for another two months, until the shuttling in itself became a way to keep the audience on their toes. He was granted a final wish, from the producers, that is; he was allowed to deliver his own memorial ("Like Donne!" a writer cried) and allowed to choose it—that searing encompassment of rest that closes Revelation 7. He recited the verses live, from the surrounding white of his hospital bed, full face, and managed to milk all three for a minute apiece.

So many additional viewers were pulled in toward the end that there was some consideration given to granting him a remission from the cancer he was dying of (kept vague, for the bedridden, but meant to be of the liver, since that could be painless) and restoring him to the show in a lesser yet more overseeing sense—perhaps as a personality of the sort once used on radio soaps, able to fuse and speed up narrative bridges with a few comments from his study. It would have been an opportunity to develop a light-handed touch that had never been seen on the medium—"Speaking here from heaven," somebody once said, imitating his voice, with a glimpse of the perspective Poppa John envisioned—and it was an opportunity he was looking forward to. But then

it was felt that the viewers had come to depend upon
the plodding daily pace and doing their own sorting;
it gave them just enough to think about.

Besides, a test had to be made, someday, it was
felt, to gauge how the loss of somebody of his status
would be borne by a loyal, if not addicted, public;
and it was also felt, over and above this, that it would
somehow weaken his authority as a character, not to
mention the "creditability" of the show, if he were
allowed to survive, *blah blah blah.*

None of them dared mention the weight of his
accumulated power. It threatened every one of them
and it threatened their jobs.

He was asked to participate in some of these
final sessions, being essentially his own creator, and
sat like a condemned man waiting to hear the date of
his execution. There was more than a thread of
theme to tie his remission to, as someone pointed out;
after all, this was *Poppa John.* When Poppa John
gave advice, which was his function on the show,
he always quoted from the Bible. Would his God
let him down now, in his need? It was one of the
younger fellows who had just started reading Psalms.
Quoting from the Bible was something Poppa John
had appropriated from his grandfather, though not
crassly; it sprang from him during his first walk-
through on the set and won the approval of the
writers—lapsed Catholics, former rabbinical stu-
dents, and assimilated Protestants from the Midwest.

His demand for fidelity to the Scriptures,

rather than secular saws, such as "Cleanliness is next to godliness," was the unspoken force, he felt, that gave Poppa John such clarity as a character and caused him, if it were so, to stand out from the stew. Underneath every phrase and every on-camera move was a galaxy of Biblical truth. His final wave, given substance by his underlying thought (he hadn't spoken for a week, to wean people from his voice, which was distinctive and his strength), wasn't meant as a farewell, but as a greeting toward the Creator he'd soon face.

He felt galactic and immeasurable in his dying, especially as he practiced it at night in bed, beside Celia, with his shoulder blades over New Jersey and the Carolinas, his lifted knees the Rockies, his hair swirling in the ocean waves, imagining all the eyes fixed on this picture of him across that curving stretch of continental space, and prayed that merely a portion of the massiveness he felt might be conveyed. And on that day, as he finished the wave, with only a hint of its former flourish, the presence of his grandfather suddenly hovered over him in a suffocating crush, and then the ruby light on the camera went off and the lights on the set came down. Dead now. He felt he'd internalized an enormous screen (visualizing all those from coast to coast going off) whose disappearing dot of light sank deeper into him until it nearly vanished, and then it began trembling, as if in a struggle, and finally flew outward into infinity with a force that left him shaken.

What in God's name had he been trying to do, and where had his grandfather come from?

He wrapped the hospital sheet around him and went into a rest room to wash off the pale pancake that Poppa John's ruddy complexion had faded to, and felt his hands scrubbing a face that wasn't his. Poppa John's. True? He looked up, catching the moment in the mirror, and examined the face in the way that only decrepit old people do, as if to read the number of days remaining in it. And then experienced, as he stared, a taste of— The taste that every actor, confined within a role, has at one time or another after the curtain falls: of resurrection, an entire new life; its potential glory, and the other, darker side, depending on the role and the show, as with one's own life. For afterlife outside the theater could be an Inferno, too, in the alternations passed through, if you were a king onstage and then walked out a back door to take the subway to your twenty-dollar-a-month Bowery flophouse room.

"Poppa John," somebody had said then, and tapped on the door. "Everybody's waiting. We have a party planned for you."

"Oh, my goodness, you would," he said, as if it were Celia.

"Pardon?"

"I'll be right there!" he said as Poppa John.

"We're waiting."

He wrapped the sheet like a toga around him and stepped out. There were more than fifty of them—cameramen, light and sound and studio technicians, engineers, set directors, propmen, costumiers, actors and actresses who weren't on the show or taping that day, some of them even with their children—seated around a long table they'd formed by laying solid flats over sawhorses down the open center of the sets. These were all in a dimness, as if being struck. A pair of fresnels lanced down, with crossing beams, to each end of the table, and a stagehand coming down a stepladder, from the one he'd adjusted, paused, with a questioning and expectant look. The look was in everybody turned to Poppa John and could go, he understood, in the direction of festivity, or toward the maudlin hugging cliquishness of theater people pulling out the stops among themselves offstage.

" 'My king! my Jove! I speak to thee, my heart!' " he cried, entirely Falstaff, and pulled a magnum of champagne from a cooling bucket close (while in an area of his inner vision a stair-step crack appeared across a panel of ice) and drank straight from the bottle. "Thank God I'm not the host!"

Poor opening ploy that the champagne soon soothed.

He stepped up on the curb at Fifty-first, noticing at Fifty-third, to his right, a lit gap that seemed a source opening out on a breeze, and there was a tremble of hesitation in his step as he was tempted by the thought of Design Research. Too expected, something elegant for the house. There was nothing he had in mind for her, or had put off buying —he'd always bought for her on impulse—but assumed there was something particular she wanted to make sure he had, just now, from her attitude. A final souvenir?

None of the effects of Poppa John's end on him and Celia were mentioned, of course, in the cover feature or follow-up. The pieces seemed to array themselves on the cramped, chopped pages in a plane as depthless as the medium they reported on. No different from most of the rest in that supermarket weekly, which, though, sometimes managed to rub the colors of an actor's real self into an otherwise empty character presently in tow. The one point that he'd stuck to throughout the negotiations with his agent was that Celia be included, and the feature was a romantically distorted version of how they spent a "usual" day in their Murray Hill apartment, without the lights or cameras or interviewers present, or the threat of that landlord who hoped to have their place removed from the rolls of the rent-controlled. The piece implied that Shakespeare and Mark Twain and Moravia were read there every day, since he'd pulled them out that afternoon; and even assigned to his and Celia's fictional bliss a stray black cat that had appeared outside their door just before the interviewers arrived, and had raised such a havoc with his hay fever it had to be put out in the street the same day.

It nestled against his beard on the cover, rather than Celia, and made him sneeze just to see it. He'd tucked the issue away between some books in an embarrassment so raw it gripped at his rectum. They'd made mention in their choppily merry prose of his training and work as a classical actor, his roles on Broadway and off, his career on the radio, begun under Orson Welles during his Mercury Theatre phase, and something of the growing importance of Poppa John to the structure that the show now had, though largely in the way in which he related to the characters who remained or were being added (a diagram was provided), and then two paragraphs about his trademark, the wave, which even three-year-olds were familiar with and could do.

The interest of the interviewers seemed to narrow down to the wave and its origins, and then a strobe flash erupted from far and near, burning different-sized coronas of color into his vision, while he repeated it for them as many times as he could muster. He said it was a version, in slow motion, of a wave he'd done in a musical in the thirties, dancing the black bottom, and went, raconteur style, into the state of Broadway then, when actors were actors and not merely personalities, and professional dancers a dime a dozen, so that the loose-limbed agility of his long legs, an aberration, had not been a liability, but had served him for once in good stead, while they stared back with the blank look of impatience and then asked another question about the wave.

And what was there to say about it? He was facing an earnest young man who said "the staff might rewrite me quite a lot" and an acrobatic woman photographer who asked as many questions. Perhaps the two of them kept at this because they knew the wave would sign and seal his end, and so in a way were foreshadowing that, and preparing his audience. He was sure the publication worked in collusion with the networks; they'd brought up several matters that only the publicity department could have supplied them with.

The man said, "I'm supposed to interview you, yet give a sort of overview of your life and work. I've never done anything quite like this. Seems a tough job."

Poppa John mentioned what was particularly significant to him about the role, from the day he'd tried out for it, which he'd been saving for this interview; how he'd felt at home in the name of Poppa John the moment he'd heard it, because of his grandfather's interpretation of the verse in Matthew: *And call no man your father upon the earth: for one is your Father, which is in heaven—* that it was meant literally. And so he'd grown up with names like Pop, Poppa, Grampop, and the like, since Daddy (and thus Dad) edged for his grand-father too near to *Abba*, which translated, in its traditional sense, nearly exactly as Daddy, or perhaps closer to "Dads," as it was used now. His grand-father was even wary of Papa, Poppa John said, and winked, since that was a name for the Pope. He grinned and the flash went off.

"I see," the man said, and made a note.

"Now, the exact verse the old fellow was refer-ring to was Matthew 23:9." He paused to allow the interviewer to note that. "It was surprising to me— not so much at the age I was then, of course, as later —to think how his influence had reached into even our lives at home, here in the city, such as they were lived then."

He'd planned to go into some of that life for the first time in this interview, but, now that the moment was here, couldn't. Instead, he quoted the verse again, which he had, along with hundreds of others, by heart, and made sure this time that it was written down.

"When you consider how briefly I knew him, it was amazing the amount of times I heard him bring that up in conversation, especially if talk of the family was involved, though he did talk about the family quite a lot, and it was usually on family matters that I was with him. I've often wondered how he'd look on me now. Given my profession and the medium it's carried on in, I'm sure I'd be a dis-

appointment to him, though I wouldn't go so far
as to say he'd disapprove, considering what I get
across, if he were here to remark on it.

"He was absolutely intransigent, that man, but
a beaut! If it weren't for his standards, so impeccable,
and the life he lived under them, then there wouldn't
be a Poppa John around to talk about, or at least not
as we know him. And if it hadn't been for Poppa
John, I think I can say without involving myself too
much in pride—I think my producers would back
me up on this, and most of the writers—I think I
can say that the show that came to form around him
wouldn't have the quality or tenor that it has to this
day. My grandfather's hand is seen in that."

"What would you say your basic role on the
show has been?"

"To keep alive the fading artifact of casual
encouraging talk. It's an art that's going from us.
Simply as such, it couldn't stand alone, or not with
any enduring impact. It proceeds out of a galaxy
of . . ."

The quote from Matthew, in the interview as it
appeared, was transmogrified worse than in a modern
paraphrase of the Bible. It turned up in a manu-
factured quote, with no reference to Scripture, by
a marvel of oversight, or editorial verve. An "elderly
man in his boyhood" had pointed out "something
colorful and intriguing that stayed." The arrogance
of such pasteboard prose! His grandfather wasn't

mentioned. None of the quotes that he'd weaved for weeks ahead with such care, in order to say exactly what he wanted to say, were used. They put quotation marks around a line he'd spoken as Poppa John on one of the shows ten years ago, as if it had come from his mouth, and not a discarded script, fresh on the day of the interview.

He'd had reservations about doing the thing in the first place, putting aside Celia, and the light he wished to have shed on her, but had been prodded by his producers (he hadn't mentioned this to her) to go ahead with it. And the producers' prodding in the opposite direction had probably brought about the apology that came, via his agent, before he'd even consented to the interview. Which he should have recognized for what it was—the consort of them maneuvering to use him for every last penny they could squeeze out—besides being unmoved. And when he saw the piece, taking it in in mad-eyed strafes at a Broadway newsstand, in an inky reek that returned with the slightest tending of his mind toward that moment, his worst reservations were confirmed, and he felt such a sick slide of shame it was as if he'd been dragged through an afternoon of the tackiest low life Broadway can offer, if not through the grime and wrinkled wrappings and hacked dollops themselves that he saw, as he glanced away, down in the gutter.

The manhandling of his grandfather was bad

enough, but the way they'd stitched in Celia here
and there, as if in afterthought, was inexcusable,
when he'd set up almost everything he'd said so
that she'd appear as his source of development and
inspiration, as she was—his mentor and muse. He
thought of hiding the magazine from her, but knew
that the sooner she saw it, before others did, and with
him there, the better.

"They haven't done you justice at all," she
said, when she'd finished, and turned to him. "They
don't make the least mention of how much of you
went into the making of Poppa John."

Besides their coverage of his wave, an inordinate
amount of words went into his beard, which was
there anyway in every photograph—pure white, or
doughnut white, as he thought of it, perhaps in
some association with his grandmother's powdered
doughnuts, which he could eat a dozen at a time, and
had been ass enough to admit. They mentioned
how, in spite of the neatly manicured trim the beard
was kept in (performed every other night by Celia,
their secret, and one he was pleased he'd kept from
their prying claws), only a half inch from his face,
it nevertheless reminded some viewers of Santa
Claus. Not the sort of valedictory one lingered over
with particular pride, after a career like his (another
grip of shame that made his face feel waxed), or
even cared to have come to mind, ever.

Actually, they had said *St. Nicholas.* Apparently

good former Catholics themselves. Exactly the sort
that formed a cloying encampment around whatever
was of individual value in one, in that it couldn't be
cast within their norms, and so kept that value from
view.

Ideologues.

He turned west on Fifty-seventh, toward Universal Pictures, and stopped outside a bar whose
name seemed compounded mostly of *M*s and *N*s.
He hadn't said to Celia today, as he'd had to lately,
that he wouldn't drink; she'd become intolerant of
his drinking, the more unpredictable it had become,
as it had. A man dressed fit for the Philharmonic
came out of the door, calling something over his
shoulder, and then stepped back, surprised behind
his horn-rims, when he saw Poppa John; and then,
with hardly a pause before he walked off, dipped
and did the wave, *his* wave. Poppa John did it back
at him and stood and watched his black-coated back
head west along the buildings among the crowd. Did
a man of that age and bearing, in this city, actually
watch the soaps?

The bar looked like a house, with a bay window
bowing out from it and shingles above; a rough plank
door, fitted with a small high window, like something
from Hawthorne, gave off an earlier century's sturdi-
ness. He pushed it in and, after an entry like an

airlock, saw another like it, but without a window, and in the move against his conscience felt his lungs constrict, as if the difference from the street were of actual atmospheric pressure, and had to breathe in a pant to get at his pinched breath as he went through it and ran into a bar—its padded edge under his hands—in the darkness. Stumblebum won't get served.

His sun-blindness began to give in chinks. The bar U'ed to his right into a cubbyhole of a room, plain and planked, where a half-dozen tables basked in faint light from the bay window. Some couples sat at them, and an older woman, alone on a bench at the back, looked as if the man he'd met outside had just walked out on her. There was a tinkling pulse of Vivaldi around his twitching ears.

He went down the bar, across its end, where a big beam wound with hawsers held a carved, beaked creature—the figurehead from a prow—and around to the other side, facing the door. Something above seemed to focus his attention down on the bar and the business of drinking, or the bottles, which were lit from underneath with an orangy glow, and he looked up and saw a rack with ropes and oars and nets and other nautical matter in it. There was a small hull and a harpoon above the woman on the bench, and a model of a fully-rigged sailing ship on a shelf, with sails bellied out in an imaginary wind.

A young man in a sailing jersey came out of

the shadows and said, "Merry Christmas," and the feeling that Poppa John hadn't quite placed, of New England mainstream WASP, was around him, like a portion of Martha's Vineyard transplanted—a fussy, polished clutter that could, with a flick of the wrist, go gay.

"Could I offer you a cup of our special holiday rum punch," the young man asked.

"A Campari soda, please."

"It's on the house." Not to be daunted; hardly old enough to buy, it looked, with streaked blond hair and a mahogany tan of the sort that comes from a bottle.

"It might nip too deep, lad," he rasped, approximating Long John Silver, or at least Beery's version of him. No response. It was the kind of movie you expected every child had seen. And then, feeling the airy lightness of no sleep, he said, "No, no, on second thought, just soda."

"Just soda?"

In his unease, Poppa John was ready to mention his age, his stomach, the day (which brought a flood of images of what he had to do yet down over him), and realized his mouth was opening on speechlessness; that block. Then fingered among the bills in the envelope and laid down a twenty, in his need to say it wasn't a matter of money. And then nearly picked it up to substitute a five. Without work to give substance to time, the most insignificant act became fraught with open-ended possibilities, as if the dailiness of simple decisions had taken on, in a nod away from them, life-and-death dimensions. How could he be expected to shop?

A snouted dispenser gurgled the liquid into his glass, over ice cubes, with an underlying hiss that peppered the bill on the bar beside with miniature droplets. He stared at them and at the spangled array of their eruptions haloing his glass, his sensibilities set at neutral, until his change came, and then moved to the end of the bar, against the wall—he was the only one not at a table—and sat on a stool, attaining the next best state to invisibility. A tuner on the top of a tall cabinet across the way was the source of the Vivaldi, or a composer like him, an early-eighteenth-century Italianate spirit, with that pulsing tonal rapidity that could stop on a dime. *A Toccata of Galuppi's.*

"Dust and ashes!" So you creak it, and I want the
  heart to scold.
Dear dead women, with such hair, too—what's become of all the gold
Used to hang and brush their bosoms? I feel chilly
  and grown old.

St. Nicholas. Hemingway was too obvious to the older viewers, and to the young, who didn't read and seemed to live by a looser code than Hemingway ever imagined, without a trace of the guilt that killed

him, and who weren't conditioned any more to
having his image stride full-front out of a picture
magazine every few months—to the young, of no
account. Acatalepsy. That old-fashioned notion that
real knowledge is only probability, not certainty,
had come full circle: now nothing was certain, because you didn't dare question anybody's right to
hold forth on any opinion he had, no matter how
arcane, as if it were knowledge, or the truth, when
such truth often buried even the obvious. The kilter
of bars.

An ancillary idea then lit: *You can't do any
more to people than what you've led them to believe
they can accept.*

An actor, a case-hardened barfly who'd got to
know Hemingway in Key West, told Poppa John
that he walked exactly like Hemingway, with an uneasy busyness about the legs that a trained observer
might detect as a weakness, in spite of the roll of his
walk. Which was a weakness Poppa John had to correct in himself, when he played Falstaff, by walking
stiff-legged and swinging his feet (which had a ten-
dency to toe-in) out in wide arcs. The actor said that
with a beard, which Poppa John didn't have then,
and a few touches of makeup, plus a different comb-
ing of his hair—now a mane of yellow-white rayed
back from his liver-spotted forehead—he could pass
for Hemingway; the actor-barfly insisted. They
were in repertory that summer in Connecticut. *All's*

Well, King John, Lear, and a semi-musical that made even less of that puff about Kate and Petruchio.

Later that summer, Poppa John let his beard grow out for the first time, for his final role, Lear, and it came in nearly as white as now. Then he and the actor went on a two-day pub crawl of New York, Poppa John allowing himself to be cajoled into his role after a few hours, with the actor at his side like a wild-eyed sycophant, gabbling on in a Spanish accent. Two columnists later had it that Hemingway had been in town with a new book, trying to travel incognito with a bullfighter.

Poppa John had kept on Floridian sunglasses to cover his blue eyes.

What many bystanders found unbelievable in him as Hemingway was actual, as attested to by a record the actor had of Hemingway reading (which Poppa John's senses, like any good performer's, had picked away at in order to find the flaw that gave him entry into the man): the high excited quality of his voice and its upper-palate impediment—"Weww, wet's have a whiskey, fewwas"—which, in itself, had brought Poppa John up against situations that still had him wondering how Hemingway had survived all those years in bars.

The deception had seemed a lark at the time, more fit for one's twenties, and the last of this sort of mindless cruelty that Poppa John was party to. It was the summer of 1952, and when he later heard stories about the peculiarities of mind that Hemingway was going through then, just before publication of *The Old Man and the Sea*, he realized how it might have affected Hemingway to have seen a story about traveling incognito in New York—a further blow toward disorientation—and Poppa John suffered for it. And suffered worse, in retrospect, after he learned, a decade later, what the self-christened Papa had been brought to at the end by his own credo and self-sufficiency; and would suddenly feel (for a character taken on isn't ever discarded) the double barrels of that shotgun in adjustment against his forehead, and nowhere else in the doorway to turn to.

He shook his head. A simple delicate song spun to its end.

He and Hemingway were of an age, born just before the century turned. Poppa John was a couple of years younger, and taller, something over six feet, presently, down from six-foot-four, due to the shrink of age. His own middle name was Ernest. He'd probably had as many eyes on him as Hemingway ever had on his prose. His face, though, was too big-nosed and blurry to pass for Hemingway's, he believed, too malleable to emotion and circumstance, with none of the definition bitten into every inch of it that decisions over separate words, and the turns of meaning that they could take within a phrase, wrought on a face.

He glanced into the mirror beside him, to check on this, and saw a grizzled old man in a beret.

He hadn't mentioned, to those interviewers, the convolutions that a role could lead to (like underground burrows whose connections could never be traced), and particularly one lived in so long; or the accommodations he'd had to make in his off-camera life to cope with the growth of Poppa John. He became so scrupulous about everyday details that Celia's patience sometimes wore thin. "Just decide, Poppa John," she'd say. "Not another silent meditation on the moral history of man. Shall we take a cab or a subway?"

He began reading the Bible, which he'd never done, moved not so much by the Spirit as a need to find verses to apply to situations that came up on the show. He gathered together the scripts, or plot outlines, all of them, even of the segments he wouldn't appear in, as far in advance as he could, and studied them from every character's perspective and possible slant. He bought a calfskin chain-reference Bible, which he kept, along with Strong's concordance, on a bedside table; both by now were softly worn. A beaded glass of water sat on a wooden chair beside the bed, a measure of his study in the morning light —he sipped his soda now—there to slake the parch that certain parts of Scripture brought on. He bought outlines of books of the Bible and sets of commentaries, and then a separate set of shelves to keep them on. The rooms became rounded with his study. Spurgeon was the interstitial tissue that tied it all into one.

He was invited to parties and dinners where as much pressure as the actor had put on him to be Hemingway was exerted on him to perform as Poppa John. But here the pressure was worse in a way, in that it was evident in everybody who'd ever seen him on the show, and created a prejudicial pull of expectation. Stepping out of the apartment into the street, he was never sure which side of himself to assume, and so would slip into Poppa John, since the chances were good he'd meet somebody who knew *him*. And once a character of such continual standing, whose gaps and limits are known, is established as benign, he's controllable; he won't slip into the unpredictable pitfalls that can seize your entire attention in the blind and tortuous negotiations you undergo in a real self.

The notion that he presented a carefully fashioned front for self-protection was a naïve underevaluation of the most superficial sort.

In every conversation he kept maneuvering behind his listening pose to come up with counsel for the moment, along with a verse or two from the Bible for support, which was also practice for the show; and after a year or two of this, both on

the air and off, his language started taking on a fussy
and archaic, semi-mystical cast, undercut by an old
man's broad salvos at humor (for true wit, which
he, however, had in his everyday life, he felt, or he
wouldn't be sane, takes a delicate, contemporaneous
tuning), which was Poppa John to the bones. But
without other characters familiar with his bias to
balance him off and keep him in check.

The ballooning balloon up out of its shed and
off.

Or worse, once outside the studios, Poppa John
a species of parasite, feeding off his feelings and
memory and reading and research and experience,
with no perception of the limits of its host, and growing every day (a thrilling inner glimpse of Hydra-
headed worms with multiple eyes circling with in-
creasing speed across a tender section of his intestines
to find a way out, causing a crazy-bone sensation in
the pit of his stomach) with Poppa John's apparent
need to placate or bring under control every person
that came within his ken. *Ken.* The baggage of that
language, still. And yet, for all that, as a man to meet
among men, beautiful in presentment, as Hamlet
might say: an orchid on a blasted stump.

Some days ago, when Celia was out, he sat in
the living room in his chair, which was a shade of
blue that seemed to resonate at the faintest ray of
sunlight on it, a blue unmatched anywhere in the
apartment, except for scattered spines of books that

appeared to enter into its resonance in a distant chord—he sat, in a vigil he'd fallen into now that he was home most days, with Verdi or Shostakovich or Bach or some other heavy playing low beside him, and watched as the sun went down, pulling its wedge of last light along the top of the cinnamon building across the street, drawing him out of himself, as always, like a tide going out, leaving an endlessness of empty beach, with tided pools of consciousness in faint reflection, until he was as insubstantial as the light itself, bodiless, layering the apartment, the building outside, the ones beside it, and then there was the creak of the metal door and its overtones within the frame as she returned; her heels across the platelike parquet. He was trying to draw himself back, so that he'd be above the depression that the hour always ended in, rendering him dazed and numb rather than despondent (a dull ache he dreaded worse than black anger or the murderous visions of the soft-spoken morose; it was Shostakovich playing), when she whispered, just above him, "What are you doing sitting in the dark like this again?"

And he said, in as even a voice as he could summon, "It was favorable to me to be without lights."

Just like the old coot!

And then, "I've found, Celia, that this acronical watch, though not entirely pleasant—I'll admit that

—is one of the few things I can depend on to soothe me."

"Oh, for heaven's sake, look above, Poppa John! Don't be a fool, and don't use your fancy King James Elizabethan to justify what you're up to. This is how men go mad!"

The multi-nostriled snout eased into his glass and sizzled some more of the eruptive carbonation over new cubes, and he looked up to find the boy, as if drawn into his concentration, studying him with eyes that scattered back in harmonics the blue of his chair.

"It's on the house," the boy said, and smiled with the unassailable confidence of family-insulated youth, a look of Celia's.

Perhaps Poppa John's footwear had led the lad to believe he was a sea salt.

"Thank you," he said, and sipped to show his thanks, seeing his long, spatulate fingers curl away from the glass, a clue to the clumsiness that could overtake him if he weren't aligned along a character, or the contours of someone else's ways. A big marionette over emptiness, at the mercy of the dozen different directions confusion could jerk him in. Irresolute, to put it mildly. As his pursed lips, going out fishlike again to suck at the soda, proved.

These worn and ragged sneakers down on a rung of the stool, with holes over their toes, were

his way of suffering a silent martyrdom, but with
outward clues. Because Poppa John had been with
Ned—how curious to think of himself as Ned
O'Rourke! now that he'd been Ned Daley for fifty
years! Because he'd been with Ned a longer time
than any phase of life that Ned had been through, his
righteous hands held the keys to Ned's freedom. *A
wise servant shall have rule over a son that causeth
shame.* Proverbs 17:2a, to put it like an academic.

What he'd gained from those twelve years, as
these last empty months, eroding him bare, proved
true, was his study of the Bible. His everyday order
still revolved around its truth. As it had been the
source of wisdom even before it was completely
recorded, and was the source of most knowledge and
philosophy and science in the Western world since,
in the ingenious and productive battering at it that it
had provoked (for it invariably provoked a reaction), so it remained for him, in spite of its present
disrepute as literal revelation, and its verses formed
a nervelike network within him.

You could say he found it easy to quote from,
on the show and in life, because he was always acting,
as somebody had said, but he was sure that its seed
set up renewing correspondences between whatever
it was that was good in him. Then again, over the
years, it had occurred to him that his Lord might
actually be his own manipulative power over Scriptures.

He tended to avoid the controversial sayings of Christ—*I and my Father are one . . . I pray not for the world, but for them which thou hast given me* (which were, after all, more evangelistic than problem-solving)—and the book of Romans, and drew mostly from the Old Testament, from Psalms and Proverbs in particular. Perhaps his single richest source, for its down-to-earth advice, was Proverbs, and this emphasis, to go by the letters he received, was appreciated by rabbis, who liked to hear the truths they taught emerge out of the TV.

He didn't exclude the New Testament, though there was plenty in it he felt it best to avoid, considering the running disputes about it between churches and the different factions within them. He became so rigorous in his accuracy to it that the writers were reluctant to bring it up, as his understanding of it grew, and put the matter back into his own lap. He could work it in as he saw fit. Improvise, practically. So the New Testament became the basis of his study. He had to know it inside out, he felt, for everything he implied or quoted direct to arrive with the right authority.

Some saw him as possessed. Others, as endearing but a fool. Mad. An eccentric. Eccentrically mad yet somehow endearing. A dupe. To be excused. An offense to himself and humanity, in a few cases, though these would have to be ranked as the most severe. Somebody once said to him that he'd like to believe in God, but it was a shame He hadn't spoken to anyone sane in fifteen centuries. There were always those. Indeed, if anybody thought He'd recently spoken to him, he might well be insane, since He hadn't spoken to anybody, period, for more like twenty centuries. His revelation was complete.

Only one person ever said to him, "Even the devil can quote Scriptures." Celia, of course.

He approached the Bible as a handbook for his role, but there were times when the separateness of it—to have its bulk in his hands to read from whenever he wished, whatever his intent, not to mention its message—opened in its immensity in him, and a verse would veer into another perspective and take on the sparkle of italics, shifting down past pages beneath, as if past dimensions it confirmed as it went, while words around flew aside, leading him to a depth he felt he could never return from, where he'd be drawn entirely in and washed over; a trembling and thud of his heart in the presence of this potential, which sometimes remained after he shut off the light, following him down to the border of sleep, where, more than once, just as he was slipping under, a voice whispered, "Ned."

The voice had the quality of his mother's, or intonations like hers, unemotional yet imperative, and he'd lie awake while beams of feeling passed through his back and forehead, and try to compose some prayer, as he had when a boy in the furnace room, that would placate the anger that seemed to spread beyond the bounds of any human being, and set up a static in the room. Or this might have been the effect of strain on his hearing as it strove back in time to check again on the tumbling lineaments of the flames in the furnace across the way, which he was able to confirm, then, by the patch of shuffling color projected in the corner beside him, or the lack of it—the building around ticking down through degrees of coldness toward its freezing point. Zero outdoors. And then there would come the muffled but penetrating voice of his father, after perhaps a few raps of the paddle or his gun butt on the floor:

"Ned!" The cottony contained density of this to him below. "Ned, are you awake, lad? Are you awake and up to what you're to be up to?"

These last months he couldn't sleep, or not more than an hour or two a night, and wasn't able to tell Celia about it, so that the sleeplessness had him halved; he carried inside a constant headache, an endless buzzing drowse, but was too enervated to nap. Everything felt oily or covered with grit, and all unmatched. He'd lie along her in bed at night, displaced, his hands curled against his chest, tortured like a honeymooner by the warmth of her sleeping weight, and by graphic displays of her entanglement with men who'd courted her, or her family had tried to force on her, before they were married—fevered apocryphal sights he'd been free of for decades. Then the windows would begin to glow and he'd wake with a start, alone in bed in another light, and understand that he'd overslept again.

"Any calls?" he'd call out, and "No" would come from another area of the apartment. "No. Not yet." So he'd drop back in bed and pray the drop would continue down to sleep, but it never did. Then the night visions and his enervation would have him in a honeymooner's state again, that senile one.

Though they said you slept even when you didn't think you had, he knew he hadn't slept at all the last two nights, except for the hour that this morning's dream had shocked him out of.

How different from the times when he'd fought off sleep to continue with his study, and then would wake to the neighborhood birds, with his Bible over his stomach, where it had fallen, or reach for it on the bedside chair, checking his beaded glass of water, and begin again where he'd left off. She could move around and do her work without disturbing him, his concentration was so perfect, and sometimes he'd look up from one of David's struggles to find her rocking in her rocker beside the bed and knitting at something in her lap in time to her rock: the swinging swatch of finished garment in its blaze of earthy color just beyond the whiteness of the page, and the tense yarn like a lifeline leading up to it, or like a pendulum swaying upside down, which, once recognized, was what had kept the strophe and antistrophe of time to the psalm that he'd been striding through.

He had a dozen sweaters that she'd made for him like this, which discerning eyes assumed were Irish imports, and the rest she gave away, as if they were cupcakes, to whichever charity she happened at the moment to be attuned to. The means that were used to salve the guilt of the born well-to-do!

Scriptures had given him slivered glimpses into the realm of time, from the vantage of his years, where a central pureness that couldn't be described, like a note of perfect pitch, held the continual revolving of the days into weeks—into months, into ages—in balance with the compiled weight of the ages revolving beneath the particular minute of each day. This one. And more than a glimpse of that antediluvian feature of the universe which one mentioned only in a joke or a curse, or in embarrassed irony, or from behind the protective isolation of the pulpit—God.

None of this had been bequeathed to him by his grandfather, the preacher. He hardly knew the man. His mother had dishonored him by running off to the city to become an actress and then, much worse, marrying a Catholic. A carnal ally of Rome, as his grandfather might have seen it, or of the Antichrist himself, if he were of that stripe. Because of Ned's own age at the time, there was no way of his knowing his grandfather's theological tendencies. How he'd rather have them in him than most of what he had of his father! His father was a policeman. He drank. He was suspended from the force. He became involved in a criminal element he was probably involved in as a policeman. He was "taken care of" when Ned was eleven.

And now a darker strumming started under the vibrating anxiety that already halved him, and he was sure he'd soon need crackers and milk.

His grandfather was never that pleased to see them (Ned and her; his father never left the city that he knew of), but put them up when his pop's drinking made life in their railroad flat unlivable. Ned spent two weeks with his grandfather, alone, the summer his pop was killed. He carried from then an image of what his grandfather stood for, shaped by his mother's stories, rather than a real man, to be truthful. Although he remembered, with a child's burning love for a figure of authority who lives by his beliefs, his grandfather's way of speech and his walk, besides the brand of his face.

Maybe the interviewers had sensed his uncertainties about him, and maybe, over the years, Celia had, too, since there was always a tremulous sense in Poppa John of speaking as an observer, back from a boyish trip to the museum: the brush of hesitant hands over bronze. Little else left now. Except for whatever it was of his grandfather that he'd subsumed as a child, now the property of that gent in the dingy beret.

There was a glimpse of the landscape around his grandparents' farm, at the edge of that nestled New Hampshire town.

His grandfather wasn't a pietistic prude; he didn't look out from Puritan eyes on the less holy, according to society's standards, like some. He'd pioneered West with the tide of the 1850's, and had the rawboned look and calm of a dependable scout. He smoked a pipe outdoors, had a cigar after his Sunday sermon, and sometimes, in the house, took snuff, though not when parishioners were present. "Hypocrisy, Ned?" he said after an elder had left. "No, more consideration of the brethren. Well, that's what I say." He required wine to be used in the sacrament, at a time when temperance was an issue, and lost members over this, Ned heard; and heard again, and yet again, from his pop.

"Here, have some, Ned," he'd say, shoving the stout or beer, which Ned had fetched in a bucket from the bar down the street, across their wood kitchen table. "You've inherited a taste for it, I'd expect, from me and your grampop."

"It's wine he drinks, dear," his mother would say, to straighten this. "And then only at the Lord's— Only the minuscule sip that's in a communion glass, and not the gobletful you can get in a chalice."

"Ah, yes, well, you see, Ned, he's not a *priest.* Only they, the true ones of the cloth, are allowed the full token." This knowing roll of the Irishman with his inside information.

The one time Ned had heard his grandfather preach, he seemed to strike sparks from the congregation, yet the sermon felt directed at him, and he tried to imagine his pop beside him, taking it in, and then understood, in a reversal of impressions he'd never forgotten, that his pop would always be with him. It was the summer he stayed at the manse, after his pop's death, and his grandfather was so attentive to him, in a way that never wavered, that a touch of his hand could bring up tears that crazed the wild New Hampshire landscape. And then for Ned, who needed this release, to look up to his height, to the bony nobility of his head, and—

It was the look and height of Poppa John now.

He took him into the woodshed one day, and said, "Now we're going to build you a wagon."

"Where will we get the wheels for it, Grampop?"

"There." He pointed to a pile of sun-speckled boards. "And that's where the rest of the wagon will come from."

He worked at it a few hours and had a frame, planed smooth and rasped; steel rods cut with a hacksaw for axles, tin strips for bearings, and then coped circles of wood for the wheels, which he fastened split lengths of hose around, to make it "quiet as a phaeton on rubber tires." He carved *NED* into the back with a pocketknife he used so well the name seemed stamped there. They painted it together with barn paint and the next day Ned was coasting down the side of the mountain on a back road—the blur of pines and the heart-piercing redolence of bleeding pitch around—with the exaltation of possession so necessary to the young, in the only wagon that he, a city boy, ever owned.

"Oh, the old fellow lives on in me as much as the Lord himself!" he once heard himself exclaim to Celia, and was appalled to think what his grandfather would say to that.

He started to attend church after he got the role. First to the Presbyterians, which his grandfather had been, before the knotty doctrines were dropped, or the divinity of Christ left to choice; and then to the Evangelicals, then the Reformed Evangelicals (with Celia, who was bothered by absolute righteousness, always along, like a good elder's wife); and then the Lutherans and the Episcopalians, and finally, out of habit, back to Rome, where he felt most comfortable.

Until they reversed the priest and upset and Englished the Mass.

Next they'd be speaking in tongues.

Poppa John

Since Vatican II, though, he was surprised at how many of the sermons seemed basically sound, rather than those exhortations to emulate a particular saint, and to pray to him or her for help in this, or those reminders to be regular about the sacraments (that necessity to "make your Easter duty" that the boys would elbow one another about in the pews) which he'd become used to when young. If it weren't for the hierarchy and history of the Church, including those Avignon popes, and for the clear teaching of Scripture on the absolute sufficiency of the sacrifice of Christ as Christ himself performed it, once, for all time, as hammered home in Hebrews 9 and 10, then perhaps the Church might have become something that even his grandfather could have learned to countenance, as he countenanced Arminians.

A word retained from then. He'd thought it referred to the people who ran the deli on their block and were among the many objects of his father's flawless mimicry.

The True Church. He and Celia were married in it, for form's sake, and to please his ailing mother, who'd proved attached to it, or determined to be loyal in that way to his pop, and tried to be devout. And then they went their own way: Sundays with the Sunday *Times.* Until the role. Then back. Then— There was something about the Church, perhaps its Virgin worship, that captivated women. As the years passed and he began to drift away, and then flee, twice weaned, absorbed in his own studies, Celia kept going, with a zeal he assumed was meant to please him. Or was it to bring him to his senses, or to some commitment about the Sabbath, prim old deacon he, with his family altar beside their bed?

She once asked him, after he'd been up all night wrestling with the warnings in Hebrews 10, if he was becoming a stuffed shirt. Or did she say prude? Hypocrite? She went every Sunday, and sometimes got up at six for weekday Mass, but in the last year or so she, too, had fallen away.

It had occurred to him that he'd been removed from the show because of their apostasy. Or, anyway, abandonment of Rome. He looked up from his soda, around at the tables, as if to check whether anybody had caught this thought. Shameful. All heads low. Bars had become, for most, the wayside chapels and churches in which to meditate. But to start running back to Rome, merely to go, without faith, would be a tail-between-the-legs womb-crawling of the Olivier Hamlet sort that he couldn't abide. And that Celia wouldn't stand for.

The illusion of exclusiveness the old Mass gave off, the complacency of its unchangeable playing out to the end, the absence of aggressive sermons, the antiquated Latin that had passed out of use, the costumed and choreographed pageant going on as if in self-sufficiency on the inertia thrown out centuries back by Christ breaking free from earth—all the qualities of the Church that had held her in thrall were exactly the ones that were done away with by the changes in it, and finally she said she couldn't bear to go any more.

It was like watching a skeleton, she'd said recently, and he, half listening, had jumped, assuming she was referring to him in his role.

His mental equipment and nerve ends were pictorial, and when images for a part were right and linked together in sequence, they ran like a movie underneath every gesture and vocal shading onstage, drawing feelings free from memory, or whatever annex it was in which they were stored; and his own perceptions, honed fine over the years, and with pressure building up in them from lack of use, had begun to form pictures from conversations or phrases overheard, as with what she'd just said. His bones stood out as in an X ray. He couldn't move and wanted to reply, with the pained jocularity of his psychiatrist, which he sometimes tried to adopt to slip out of a corner, while he stood with his back to her, staring into their closet: You mean, like my irreproachable little nuns, all running around nowadays in designer clothes?

Love?
He drew in his lower lip and chewed at his beard in the rabbity nervous nibble that Celia hated

so, saying it made him look like a toothless and en-
feebled old fool, while he waited in the widening
calm which he was convinced, from his reading, he
and epileptics shared.

God. He was as much a present, vengeful, un-
remitting source of wrath, when not taken on His
terms, as a vague and distant God of love. *For I the
Lord thy God am a jealous God, visiting the iniquity
of the fathers upon the children unto the third and
fourth generation of them that hate me.* But the
contemporary emphasis was on love, and that was the
way people wanted Him now, if at all—as syrup.
It was in their natures to overlook a love that restrained, or held safe from Sheol, the Abyss, or
maintained limits over those it was directed toward,
as a father tells his child not to play in the streets, and
then keeps watch. They wanted syrup, when He'd
never said that if you love me you'll be overcome
with passive neutrality and mushy inarticulate emotion, but: *If you love me, keep my commandments.*

It appeared that everybody was well enough
informed on Him to know where you'd wind up if
you didn't, at the least, which implied another side
to Him, but it was that artificial saccharine confec-
tion—formed by modern theologians who were as
much psychologists and social theorists as men of
God—that Poppa John's audience wanted to hear
about, of course, from Poppa John. And hear they
did.

Poppa John

He was aware of the whoredom in this, of a magnitude greater than taking a role in the soaps to begin with, but fought for accuracy in everything he was given to say, or quoted, convinced that his scrupulousness here was his out. And there was further motivation. The supernatural appeared in everybody's life in the form of patterns and events that rose from the surface flux like a fist and defied explanation: the call from the person you're thinking of, the professional paralyzed at his desk by a letter from a schoolfriend he hasn't heard from in thirty years and mentioned to his wife that morning; the number of the friend's address is the same as the suite of offices where the professional sits chilled. Some people wanted a hook other than coincidence or psychic power or periods of apparent madness (being "freaked out," as the young had it) to hang such on, and he tried to provide that.

You couldn't disallow the implications that daily life sometimes presented by pretending they didn't exist, or by turning from them to a superficial antidote, such as TV, or any diverting realm of little dimension where such matters didn't enter, or were laughed off. They stayed and reoccurred. In that sense, he felt that the soaps, in their confrontations with the everyday mundane, had more integrity, actual and ameliorating, than the nighttime shows. And they reached women and children, who ran the households now. He'd hoped to help create an opening, a pulled thread in the fabric, that might eventually permit something of real substance to emerge.

And now this. Not only constricted by every constraint he'd ever felt from every director and writer he'd ever worked with, but now no forum. If television, in its present trends, could be considered a forum he still wanted to use.

And this darker strumming underneath to be answered to.

He looked around again, wishing there was a booth where he could hide for a while, or a bathroom in sight. When he settled into such a place, particularly if he was drinking, it felt as if his tailbone sent down roots, uniting him to the stool or booth he was in, so that it was difficult to move, much less leave, until his sequence of thought was carried to its conclusion. His bladder had to clang with demand for relief to get him to his feet, even, and that matter was disposed of with such dispatch it was as if dumb organs had dashed off to do their bothersome duty (nevertheless calling up grateful groans that they continued to work) and then were reunited with the sitting essence of him that had remained.

When he was young, during cold weather, he'd had to sleep down in the basement below their apartment to keep the furnace for their building stoked. His pop took on the job after his suspension, to help cover the rent, and they moved from the fifth floor, where they'd always lived, down to ground level, to be close to the building's innards. His pop also had to maintain two other buildings for a rental agent, and worked at night as a watchman up and down the block. He showed Ned how to check the gauges and how to lay a fire and keep it stoked when Ned was ten, still in knickers and ribbon ties, and after that it was his job.

When he was done with school, he'd come down to the basement, through the alley entrance, to the closet where he kept his shoes and a change of clothes. His pop made him carry his shoes and walk barefoot to school and back, in all but the worst of winter weather, to save on shoe leather and repairs. He was laughed at, of course, and began to stop around the corner from their place to pull on his shoes, leaning back against a brick building that was always warm at that hour, and then one day his father, looking flushed and ragged from the night, was waiting at the schoolhouse door to see if his orders were being carried out. He hustled Ned into an entry under a nearby stoop, had him grip his legs above the offending shoes, and beat his butt with his watchman's bat until it felt like a baboon's.

There was an alcoholic reek in the entry that might have come from his pop. He drank every day since the suspension, but was never stumbly or out of control, except for a few times that could be counted on one hand, and each of those times he'd beat Ned. They were probably so poor they had to save on whatever they could, including the beer brought home in buckets, which his pop might have needed to stay sane. Everybody worked then, children included, as everybody should—*In the sweat of thy face shalt thou eat bread*. If you didn't, you fell into the sort of state he was now in. His pop wasn't unreasonable or brutal, if you put aside the times he got out of hand, which were never sustained and always apologized for, with a strained tug of guilt around his tortured eyes, so they were probably that poor then. But at his age he wasn't so astute about economics, or even attuned to them, and hated carrying those shoes. It was hard on him.

He changed clothes in the closet and often stayed down in the basement, after filling the furnace and sweeping up and carrying out the clinkers that had cooled overnight, until he was called for supper, or heard the thumps on the floor that meant him. The loaf of brown bread lying half sliced in the seething glow of gaslight on the smooth-worn table. The covered tub behind him, where chickens waiting to be plucked sometimes hung from their claws. The icebox in the corner, with a shotgun leaning against the wall beside it. The leaden figure on the crucifix above the hallway door. A service revolver on the top of the icebox, or on the chair, through that door, beside his parents' bed, or sometimes slung from its holster belt over his pop's shoulder, though always put out of the way for meals.

Only the murmured grace and the objects around remained the same from four floors up. His mother's attitude and temper were new and arrived in a voice, raised out of proportion to the moment, that he'd never heard. Her silences, which were worse, weighed on him like a blanket of blue. His pop hadn't allowed her to return to the stage once they were married, and in their circumstances her ambition, and her resentments about its being thwarted, returned.

She'd done well for a while in music-hall comedy, which wasn't quite burlesque, from her manner of phrasing (and what he himself was able to learn, later, going through her clippings), and in melodrama when it was still a respectable form, having inherited some of its posturings and histrionics from men like Booth and Kean. She said her beauty was ruined. She once clawed her cheeks, bandaged her face like a mummy, and went out shopping for the neighborhood to see. In a rage that must have been bottomless, but under terrible control, she cut his pop's two uniforms into shreds the size of postage stamps with her nail scissors. She often said, "I want you to stop your commerce with that element."

And his pop would say, "Which one?"

He said he'd been suspended because he knew

too much about certain goings-on in the department. When she asked him to explain, he'd set his mouth and lift his chin as if in brotherhood, or professional silence.

He went off to irregular, clandestine meetings, his revolver stuck in his belt behind his spine, and some nights a pair or group of men would come to the alley entrance and talk with him there in whispers.

So his homelife had given him the heart, the internal training, for the sordid domesticity essential to the soaps. Poppa John. His embodiment of him was so assured, in a way that wasn't offensive, because he never had to consider bettering his father. No, he led a disciplined, artistic life, based on dedication and daily order, and this had been reinforced over the years by regular habits. Except for some slips these last months. His early training with Barrymore and Skinner, and then Welles, had given him standards that were alien to present-day actors, some of whom had trouble understanding what he was up to, and he'd been referred to by a few, and by critics otherwise unsympathetic to his style, as aristocratic. It was the tone and bearing he brought to every role and room he walked into, and had nothing to do with him.

Throughout his term on the show, from the

1950's to the present, from loose and squarish suits with padded shoulders to the look of now, he'd always made sure he was provided with the best clothes in the current fashion. If they didn't appear quite good enough to him, he wore his own. People who took characters on the stage or television seriously were the kind who paid an undue amount of attention to clothes. An actor who came from Toronto told him that the U.S. was five years ahead of Canada in style, and New York approximately that far ahead of the rest of the U.S., and this Poppa John took in, not just as information, but as a call to be unassailable in how he dressed. Most actors' eyes are busier than anybody else's touring exteriors, and this man had been sent, Poppa John felt, to sharpen his own.

The dress, of course, didn't render him the person he was seen as; indeed, there were times when his proper surface veneer seemed to be painted from the inside with buckets of blood.

And aristocracy wasn't something he could shape on his own or consciously work at, even if it were what he wanted most. But once seen and accepted, it was there to refine until it glinted out from the ranks of those he stood among. It was a gift, a gift pure and simple, which work and wear had rubbed over the years into an appearance of being natural, and his own. He hadn't inherited it from bloodlines, and it wasn't in his upbringing, or environment, certainly, and if it came directly in any form it was perhaps as a legacy from his grandfather, in the way in which that legacy rose out of his mother's poised and self-contained assurance of trusting to her instincts.

Women remained the same and had from the beginning, since Eve. You only had to look into the eyes of any portrait or photo from any age to see that. Open lines back to life, with an outlook to-ward— Whatever more lay ahead. It was men who changed. You could see it first in this country in the photographs from the Civil War. There was a look in the eyes of the soldiers, young and old alike, North and South, whenever caught in repose, that struck you as new, and perhaps it was in those battles of brother against brother that the battle lines of the future were drawn. Fraternal betrayal. Mistrust. Matriarchal households. The loss of an order. Then the backlash as the century swung: more factories, bigger machines to get operating right, brandy and cigars after dinner, nights out with "the boys"; murky meaningless poetry, the spread of brothels— pornography's further distancing.

The twenties and thirties were another phase of it, looking into eyes, all the way up to the present, where men were acting out the compiled shock of having sacrificed too much to change. Widening riots and assassinations. This present cruel war. The pull there to win, because of this country's power

(such a male entrapment), and the repellent force of
its basis, which had sent so many of the young off to
neutral places, and left an impression of cowards in
skirts. Until, in a further reaction, the idea of same-
ness had arrived.

Brothers and sisters, indeed.

If you really thought that men and women were
basically the same, except for obvious physical dif-
ferences, then you ought to ask any homosexual.
There wasn't the confident set deep back in the eyes
that there was once, and he suspected that a direct
look of his father's sort would now wilt most men.
Not that he was his father, or would want to be, but
he was his son and had seen the change achieve a peak
that had brought it into common currency. You
didn't need to be an expert to see certain trends, and
the media's power was in instilling images: the
neutering of the many by the few.

Any weakness or trait that could be played upon
to make a sale would be so used. He'd seen the watch-
works from the inside. He'd been a part of the crew.

The way that men and women were the same
was in their hearts, equally filled with alibis and
deceit, and if you couldn't see that by looking into
your own, then you were either blind or a liar, or so
self-deluded as to deserve pity (since lack of discernment eroded not only the power to perceive
but your humanity) for being such a fool.

His pop would say, "If most men's lives
were thoroughly looked into, most'd deserve death.

Murder one. And if there's some haven't accomplished what they'd like to, it's only because they haven't the guts to. There's no man so sweet there's nothing foul on him. Which isn't said from seeing, as I do, mostly the dregs and scum. And, anyhow, scum floats on top."

His mother would have her back to him, enduring this, or would say, "That's no way to speak with a child present, Seamus."

"This 'child' had best learn what's out there before he steps forth. And that stepping he might soon have to do."

He narrowed his rust-lashed eyes to impress this on him, and she swung from the counter, her face flushed above her lacy collar, her hair hanging in loops from the coiled pile that seemed to draw up her eyebrows, her lip lifted over her pretty teeth, her whole self trembling in this state, and said, "Why, you sound just like my— Like his grampop! Oh, *men!* All of you! Oh! Oh, *screw!*"

He tended to live down in the basement. The furnace was always there as his excuse. He assumed that songs like "Old Black Joe" and "Steady Old Ned" were meant for him. And the furnace, wrapped at its joints with asbestos, massive in the blackish room, trembled around the turbulence of burning deep in its bulk in a way that drew him. The dense content of coal—all in a weighty negative, all in

blackness—that the furnace could consume to support the night. The art of laying a fire of consistent
heat so there was no waste, or unnecessary work to
go into. The bake over his face from the orange-red
coals when the door was banged back to bank it
again; the scrape of the scoop at 2 a.m. The pillow
on the cot that smelled of his pop's pomade, from
his daytime tending and sleeping here.

And the steady burning accompanied by a
sound as of a driving, shifting wind throating
through the firebox and flues, so that if he closed his
eyes on the cot he could imagine from the noise and
the drafts over his face that it was April outdoors. It
was here that he first read Shakespeare. He found the
volume on their shelf of books upstairs and brought
it down. He set a shaky table in the corner, where
the projection of the fire shuffled in bars inside a
square along the wall, and set a chair he found in the
storeroom up to it, and had his niche. He lined his
books across the table in the order that he chose to.

First he did his schoolwork, and then opened
the bulky volume that absorbed him into the lives
of its kings and queens and clowns, and the castles
and landscapes that they walked in—all created by
people speaking, but in a language that was made of
richer material than the one for the usual world.
The resonating tumblings of the flames in the furnace
behind were like undertones of the vast and omnis-
cient voice that every other voice on the pages rose
from. Constellations of a sun. The radiating heat of

the burning coal that penetrated his clothes to his very substance.

The sooty sulfurous smell that was always there, and the grit that came to overlay whatever wasn't covered with cloth, permeated the words themselves, as though they'd been fashioned in a smithy's realm, a black and red kingdom, and he could never read passages afterward without that atmosphere, along with a catch of odor at the back of his nose, reaching across the years to surprise him. Besides a wave of the warmth that seemed to hold him unmoving and whole. This was home to him when he was called in his heart to it in its real sense. This was the place that his affection for the art, and his closeness to it, came from.

And then to go upstairs, or outside, brimming with those words like a vessel that could spill, to see everything that he looked upon transformed—a tree, chapeled in the moonlight against a warehouse, suffused with Shakespeare and Shakespeare rearranged by the branches of the tree—all partaking of another dimension, yet each even more its essence in this mellow new light, until he became so filled with feeling that imagery went rushing out of him in glittering planetary expulsions. And then he was ready to read again. Not emptied, but wanting to be changed and to see the world revealed in change, from the tiniest pebble he might pick up, to his parents as they went together to their bedroom and closed the door on their further, personal mystery.

Poppa John

And there was another intimation from then
that came both when he was awake and up through
the hatch of dreams, like those flies that would appear in the basement in the worst of the cold, from
wherever it was that was their place of resurrection:
that he himself had written something there (perhaps from all that homework done), turning over
page after page through the night to the tones of the
furnace going at its peak, while its heat through his
clothes rendered him a body so defined it seemed to
glow in the dimness and shed the steady light that
he worked by.

A prisoner to his father, in a sense, and his iron
rule. And yet—

Poppa John looked around, feeling eyes on him,
and saw the woman at the back bench, alone, trying
to act as if she hadn't been staring, and then looked
into his drink again. —Yet he loved him. The cubes
appeared to swell and spangle at this. You only had
one father. And no matter what sort of father he
was, or what the manner of his leaving, or what age
you were when he went, once he was gone you were
without a father. No grandfather or family friend
could hold the same profile against the panorama of
the stars.

His pop was respected in the neighborhood and
was called upon to settle minor disputes. He was considered scrupulous in his personal dealings and fair

with a set of facts. He didn't abuse his strength or
city connections. Nobody dared pick on his boy
while he was alive, and after he was gone the work
he'd set for Ned in the basement had built Ned up,
and he'd begun to take on his pop's height and
breadth, so he'd served him even there. His mere
existence made Ned what he was.

You might as well give your parents every
credit you could while your tongue still moved.

And it was in the basement that he'd been released into the life that he'd follow, led by his mother's
example—who, though, for her part, turned her back
on the stage the day his father was killed. And there
were the times when his pop's garrulous self, which
had overrun the rooms of their fifth-floor apartment,
reappeared, and then the rooms of their present
place, arranged exactly like the rooms of the old one,
took on a double depth, as if the other had been
transposed over this, and was lit at all its corners with
the sceptered light out of Shakespeare's realm.

It was his pop who first read aloud from the
plays to him (and so later made him seek the volume
out), letting his voice roll with the language that was
probably closer to his Celtic ideal than American.
He'd left his family there. He told bedtime stories
about a boy named Sean who captured more crim-
inals than the detectives in the department, because
he had plain common sense and went everywhere
barefoot, noiselessly, like an Indian.

Some nights he sang as he sat in the dark beside

the bed. Gaelic songs, or old ballads, or songs with a folk flavor, and Ned could still catch the quality of his voice as it went:

> All will be well, if —if —*if*
> [The faintness of this last!]
> Say the green bells of Cardiff.

Then his singing would trail off and he'd sit in silence (he'd only say he'd left his family as a young man), as if listening, and it would seem that a third person had entered the room. He'd rise then, a silhouette against the open doorway, and rise and expand until Ned was engulfed. A kiss on his forehead. Then the dense and oily masculine smell of him above, breathing yeast, as he straightened the covers and tucked them in tight. Then the silhouette moved back and for a second, struck by the hall light, became his father, drawing the third person out to him. Gone.

His retreating steps down the long empty hall, and then the door went black.

Yet he was always there. He coached Ned in his catechism and told him that if there was ever a time in his life when he would be perfectly honest, his first confession was to be that time, and made him promise that. So when Ned pushed aside the velvet curtain and pulled it closed and kneeled in dark-

ness on a wooden bench on knees that gripped and
quavered so much he wasn't sure he could whisper
well enough to be understood, with the gruff-voiced
priest on one side smelling of wine, and his father, so
he sensed, keeping him to his promise on the other,
he felt he was in the presence of God himself, and
pressure came down in probing beams that penetrated
every inch of his skin to the depths of his most
hidden secret deeds. And the more that these were
exposed, the more they seemed to multiply (it was
endless!), as he hurried and put aside what he'd
planned to say, and then began to confess all that
was now revealed to him. Until finally the old priest
interrupted. "Many of these seem venial to me," he
said, "and perhaps were best saved until your next
confession, though I do understand how you might
wish to unburden yourself. Remember, God sees.
However, if you have any truly mortal sins, you
must tell them to me now."

His pop came to his First Communion, looking
choked and stricken in a high collar and tie, and
stood under the trees that were outside the neighborhood church in those days, with a foolish grin on
his face and a glaze in his eyes that Ned took to be
from liquor. Ned went over to him, full of fear and
shame, and his pop sank down on his haunches and
took his hands. Those eyes with the foreign blue of
the sea in them.

"You'll remember this day the rest of your life,

son," he said. "You'll remember me saying this to you as I am. Hold on to what you have as of this moment! Be honest and love your God. You'll never be as pure as you are now. You're as clear as the sun in the air above, I can tell that. These leaves are clearly of God's world in your eyes. I want to hold you."

He took him in his arms, where there was a scent of pomade but no booze, and then in the harsh rasp of his heavy beard (which they called his hedgehog) against Ned's neck there was a sudden warmth that grew and ran; the ancestors in him, free of the curse of the snakes, were crying.

And then the darker strumming underneath became symphonic, fragmenting the separated halves of him, and he was back on the cot trying to disentangle himself from the quilt as his father came toward him out of shadow in a scraping slippered run. Though he'd been beaten when he'd fallen asleep, once, in his first month, this wasn't how it had happened—he'd awakened to blows across the quilt—but this was how it came; and what came was only his father's face, magnified to fill the upper basement, fixed in an expression of death, sailing at him just below the stovepipes, as if, in the tilted perspective the moment always assumed, the shiny columns of pipes were guiding his fall toward the cot (and if it came at night as he lay beside Celia, there was a snuffling breathing sound in the silence, in time to the slippers he could never see, which rose into his growing pant of anxiety), and then the deafening stomp of a revolver going off in a closed space.

He needed crackers and milk.

He poured down the soda and started buttoning to leave, the room dimming down to the area of mahogany that held his glass, and then the snout came up with its gurgling regurgitation over the cubes again.

"Rest room."

"Straight back, sir. To your left."

He went to it on liquidy limbs as patches over his back seemed to lift away and wing off, and found himself in the noisy, lighted corridor of an apartment building or business place where people milled. Was this some— Then he saw the two doors, down a ways to his left, went through one, went into the booth inside it, bolted the door, and sat down on the stool as he was.

It hadn't happened that way. He'd never seen his father use his revolver but once, in the coal bin, at a target he'd set up against the slide of coal, with Ned far back, when Ned was at the age where he had to see how it worked and had been begging him for months to shoot it. But that was how it came. Certain details, he sensed, were from the dream he'd been

7 9

awakened out of the night his father was killed, and which he'd never been able to recapture and sort, because at the moment he awoke, caught in the covers, the latch on the door across the furnace room lifted. And then the door opened enough so that he could see, in the light from the furnace, the shine of a single eye.

Whose?

He'd tried to resee it so many times since, it had become a hole he saw through. The door closed.

He tugged away his topcoat, tugged his belt loose, pushed down his pants, and took a leak.

He'd gone to the door as soon as he was able to. Then up the stairs to the alley entrance, and then back down again, silent, sensing that the person hadn't left the basement. He lay down. Then he got up, with the shuffling light shifting over him, and got a crate out of the closet that he dressed in, set it under the window by the stairs, and got up on it to see out—this window from whose bottom he'd looked out other nights, trying to identify the men who met with his father in the alley, some of whom seemed friends from the force, slow and familiar and solid in the way that his father was, and some with the flashy adolescent swagger of the sort who have to travel in pairs to flay one another into action, since there's no moral base in them for courage to build on.

No one there now. Not a misplaced shadow in the blackish-blue. Then farther down—

Somebody rattled the door of the stall and bolts of light appeared in glancing lines from above him. "Sorry," a voice said.

He put his face in his hands and leaned forward. The sounds from that night that had never left him. Farther down along the row of ramshackle barns and carriage houses a horse had stomped. Or so he had thought. Then this came again. He stood staring out but there was no movement, no footsteps, no further noise; no one appeared in the bluish-black that the gaslight of the lamp on their side street barely reached into. He put the crate back in the closet (seeing, now, down in the stall, through a gap in his fingers, a worn and ragged sneaker alight with a significance he'd never attributed to it, in the harsh exposure that always followed one of these incursions) and then lay back down on the cot. There were some distant sputs like water in the coal. But not that. He couldn't sleep, sure that somebody was still in the basement, waiting, and in the morning, when his pop didn't come home, said he was too ill to go to school.

That afternoon his pop's body was found in the abandoned factory at the end of the row of carriage houses. His wrists were wired together, his ankles wired, his head bludgeoned in, and his throat cut. His revolver had also been emptied into the back of his head.

It was the time of terrible corruption that continued through the reign of Mayor Gaynor, who

himself ended up being shot, and it was all overlaid
for him now with an oldness that appeared, each
time the incursion came, as an element brand-new:
the ramshackle barns and carriage houses had come
to resemble, in the years that had intervened, a decrepit row of buildings in a sepia photo (seen in
some book) taken outside Ford's Theater on the day
after Lincoln was shot. Like the handwritten draft
of that letter in the stone and gilt and tapestry
atmosphere of the Players Club, under protective
glass, from Edwin Booth to the shattered country
that had started to reunite around Lincoln, grieving
the grief caused by his brother, and, beneath all that,
in his scratched-in phrases on the manuscript, grieving his brother as a father grieves a son. This splen-
did man and Hamlet having to face his other side.
Flung down on the four-poster in the bedroom
upstairs.

The creative, the urge to make new and change,
suddenly gone wild.

For a year after the shooting, Kip, a friend
from the force, had his face pressed close; it was
forced in front of him, it was beside his on the
stoop, it was craning across the kitchen table, while
Kip went over and over in his earnest steady way
what an unforgivable thing this was that had been
done, so near to a man's hearth and home, and not

giving him a fighting chance; the vicious overdoing
of it, and how he and perhaps some of the other
boys would pay back in kind what was due when
they were sure of the culprits, even if it meant losing
their jobs, or worse, to do the deed—avenging angel
with his wide blue eyes that never appeared to blink,
his rugged puffy face so pitted with acne his shining
skin seemed all scar, a melt annealed, and then that
index finger he kept jabbing into whatever was close,
to make his point, the tip of it missing, so it seemed
he'd driven it up to the first joint into the table or
concrete—until Ned couldn't picture his father's
face any more (he hadn't seen him dead, and that
night had blurred the exact moment he'd last seen
him alive) and hadn't been able to since.

The face that came at him was more than a
distortion (an incubus, one man called it) and could
be claimed as his father's only from the feeling that
poured from it. All that remained, in reality, were
those eyes, with their narrowing, reddish, cunning
lashes, and the line of his lifted chin. They found
that he'd taken out enough insurance to settle the
two of them for years.

No one was sure, even now, that he hadn't been
working undercover. Or there was no one who
would say.

He'd lived with the death and the rest throughout adolescence and his twenties, and then saw an
analyst, who was shaved bald and of the couch and

Viennese school, and wasn't much help. And this was before the face coming at him had even occurred. He'd decided to try the man's witchcraft, or wizardry, as it was looked upon then, as a way of getting on Kip's case, and sorting out what could be done about him, but after a few visits understood that he wasn't going to get the kind of advice he wanted, and knew that all there was to do was to look up Kip himself. He was convinced by now that Kip was involved in the murder, if not the murderer plain.

"It was his manner," he said to the silent dome of the man at his side, whom he couldn't help turning to, though he'd been asked to try not to. "And the way he'd go through that grisly detail, staring me in the eye all the while, as if to see how I was taking the torture. He had the fractured— He had the practiced look of getting even. Even through her. And then—"

"Yes?"

But he couldn't tell this man; he stopped seeing him.

Coming home from school one day, early, he saw the bulky shape of Kip, with sunlight from the living room in a spiky onslaught behind him, come hobbling down the hall trying to get his trousers up, waving his free hand with its nipped finger, crying, "Stay back, boy! I've got the dysentery, it looks. I've been on and off the crapper since I come at noon.

Your ma is cleaning up after me, poor saint! Hurry go get me some bicarbonate."

He went for a pocket as if to get change, grabbing at his flopping braces, and then they both looked down; his feet were bare.

"It was like Hamlet," Poppa John said to the psychiatrist he finally saw in seriousness. "Like being caught inside the play while it was in full swing, and not remembering for sure what came next or how it all ended, except in a bloody mess. Or what your relationship to it was. And then having to improvise. Like that dream where you walk onstage and don't know for sure what play it is or any of your lines. But everybody was real."

"And if you'd asked them, everybody probably would have had a different version," the man said. "Like the Player Queen."

He took a leak again. This, too.

He had to say for his mother that Kip was never in the house again, that he knew of.

He'd dealt with that, too, and gone on into his thirties, and then Celia arrived, for good, spreading forgiveness back over her links with those days, and it wasn't until his fifties, when he was doing the role he was at last ripened to do now, Lear, and the fool was fastened to him with a chain from the final scene of the first act until the end of Act IV, and sometimes spoke in the tones of Lear in a perfect imitation of him, like Lear's detached and battered ego—it wasn't until then, as he turned to the little cringing figure with the voice as big as his, crouched alone with him onstage—the same spidery wizened fool who'd played the Spaniard to his Hemingway— that the face first came at him with its full force. The fool gaped and scowled, giving contours to the moment that the face from then took on, while he himself, deaf and blind to all but this, gulped like a fish in air, and then managed to make it through the scene. Then the play.

Somebody shook the door of the stall again.

He'd dealt with the face, too, until— For a while, when neither he nor Celia nor alcohol, nor any combination of them, could bring any relief, he saw a man that Celia had found who seemed to help; or the phenomenon gave out on its own. The man commended him for tracking down Kip, to resolve that for himself, which he'd done after those first fruitless sessions decades ago, when there was a possibility that Kip might still be alive. He'd traced him back to Buffalo, where he'd died of a brain hemorrhage, from drink, alone in a rented room, from the evidence. The missing finger tip mentioned on the death certificate, along with the coroner's description of his face, guaranteed that it was Kip. No one claimed the body, the coroner reported. It was burned.

He told the man this, and the details of Kip coming down the hall, and his guilt about posturing

as Hemingway, and whatever else occurred to him
that seemed relevant, and after a few months felt
well enough to quit. The face came only once or
twice a year, if that often. The man suggested he
might take a few drinks at those times, if he wanted,
to help quiet the anxiety, which was the wrong thing
to tell an Irishman, or any man, as far as that goes,
who drank for that reason to begin with, and knew it.

And then he took the role of Poppa John, and
in his second year, as he started to question the ethics
of it, and of television itself, yet at the same time
settled with more relish into the work he'd involved
himself in, the face stormed at him with more fre-
quency. It came while he was on-camera once,
fraught with the overtones from Lear, and though
he was able to finish the homily he was in the midst
of, and get through two other scenes done live (as
they were all done then), the hollow-eyed, scanning-
for-an-exit look of anxiety was there on the screen
for everybody to see. When he got home, Celia met
him at the door, and said, "Poppa John, you tell me
this instant what happened on that set today!"

She persuaded him to go back to the psychiatrist, who dealt with celebrities and professionals,
and was first recommended to her by her female
doctor at Columbia; both were on the teaching staff.
There wasn't any of the academic about him. He was
huge and hearty, a Toby Belch who wouldn't re-
quire a pound of artificial padding—his big belly

belted around the middle, and voluminous trousers shaking from there when he walked—and young then, in his late thirties. He sat directly in front of you, studying every move, his face intent on you, nodding (quaking jowls brown-black with a beard he shaved several times a day: if Poppa John had an appointment in the morning or after lunch, he was clean-shaven; just before noon or at the end of the day, beginning to bristle), encouraging and alert in a black captain's chair that bore some organizational insignia on its back and gave out cracking reports of its ultimate breakdown whenever he shifted his weight or laughed.

His gift was his sense of humor, which might be interpreted as improper levity by some, and the ways in which he used it to guide you into a moment that caused you to laugh, at an insight that was pertinent, or to an absolute laugh, so that in the eruptive seizure of it, like flashbulbs going off, you were able to see yourself with detachment from several sides. What Poppa John had never confided to anybody, and needed help with now, were those sounds he'd heard that night, which he was sure were the blows being dealt to his father. And his revolver going off.

"Did you ever check inside the warehouse?"

"Where?"

"Where his body was found?"

"No."

"How do you know you could hear anything

from where he was killed? I mean, when you were inside your building?"

"I heard something."

"I guess you did."

Silence.

"What did the police say about the sounds?"

"I never told them."

"Because they were *police*, right?"

"Exactly." This related to his mother.

Silence.

"Would you like to talk about the closet again?" The man's jowled face, neutral but for his searching eyes, hung fire for Poppa John's present response to this running joke that referred, of course, to his relationship with his father.

"Did you go inside it, Poppa John?" Celia asked; she was there with them also, after the first year of this. "I mean, the warehouse."

"Factory. I was afraid to. Then it was torn down."

"To tell the truth," the man said, "I don't know if I would have had the guts to go as far as you did, at that age." His heavy Queens accent sent furls of sparks off of his pop's voice. "You know, from that closet up to the window." He hung fire.

"It didn't occur to me. He was my father." He sounded eleven again.

"Yes, but you didn't know at the time what was up that night."

"There was the dream. I realize you don't put much stock in dreams."

"I've never said that."

Silence.

Behind the man, outside sliding glass doors, was a greenhouse where Poppa John let his eyes travel during these silences, over the potted and hanging and climbing and staked plants and ferns and flowers and cactuses there—all under bright lights, in a colorful and steamy profusion. One day they'd stepped into the office to find the man among this growth, his eyebrows raised and lips parted in a half smile, a watering pot out in one hand, the other behind him, fingers pointed down, poised as if in the midst of a dance.

"If I could have done something, anything"— feeling his money tick away and a need to fill the lull—"when I saw that eye. If I would have screamed, or run up and got the shotgun—"

"It might have been an old wino."

"—but I wasn't sure it wasn't him."

"Kip?"

"My pop. Anything I would have done might have helped him."

"Look. Think of your age then. Hindsight can be a kind of torture."

"Somebody might have heard, or the person run off and scared whoever it was in the factory. If I'd paid more attention to how Pop was acting that day, which maybe the dream was trying to warn me about, then I—"

"Or if he hadn't been a policeman in the first place."

"True."

"Look, Poppa John, er, ah, *Ned*." This was something the man often did, like stepping on a cockroach, and Poppa John wasn't sure it wasn't intentional, a part of his therapy. "You could stay in that circle forever. The thing for you to look at now is that he's dead."

"What?"

The man set his elbows on the arms of the chair and his feet came forward in a hurried pattern, as if to firm the moment, and then he leaned so that the weight of him, gathered in his eyes, went deep. "You have to admit that he's dead. You'll never see him again. You don't have a pop."

Poppa John's face froze at this, although he was able to conceal it, he was sure, and he listened in a daze to the rest that was said, letting Celia bear most of the burden of response, and then their time was up; a formal handshake, and he was out the door, in city air, in the East Eighties, and suddenly had to lean against a building and grip its bricks to keep his feet.

"That Kraut!" he cried.

"Poppa John, what is it?"

"That dirty rotten Kraut!" He was sobbing. "I know he's dead. I know I'll never see him again! But he didn't have to say it like that. He didn't have to be so unchristly cruel, the bastard!"

He stood, zipping and buttoning up, the authority of surfaces banging at his perimeters, and opened the door to find a pale man, with his jacket already removed and draped over an arm, waiting. And then had to hurry over to the urinal and use it—this, again—as the man settled himself in. He turned a faucet on and off and went out and down the noisy corridor into the dark quiet of the bar, went to his corner, and tried to pour the soda down. But propriety, curled around his condition, constricted his throat.

He needed crackers and milk.

"Sir."

The woman from the back bench was standing beside him.

"You must be Poppa John."

There was a tremulous hoarseness to this, as if she were speaking through tears, yet a satisfaction so final it nearly forced out of him: *No.* Or, for the first time: *I was.*

"I was positive it was you the moment you walked in. It seems ordained."

She was in her forties or fifties, all in tan and green, with a large green hat like a bell over the back of her burnished curls, and stared up at him from a face that looked professionally made-up, or as a Frenchwoman would (in a blended translucency nearly invisible), out of beseeching eyes so surrounded with kohl, as though dripping black, he felt onstage. "I've looked forward to this meeting for more than a decade. Could we please talk?"

He managed something about much to do.

She stepped closer and he saw, in one of her eyes out of the shadow of the hat, a shimmer that wasn't of drink, a mourner's stare; her compressed lips were quivering; her entire body seemed to.

"I'm so lonely, Poppa John, I hardly know what to do. Won't you please talk with me a moment. It's taken this long to work up the courage simply to approach you. This is the first I've spoken to a man without an introduction. I know it must seem shamefully déclassé to do such a thing in a place like this, and I suggest that we leave, if you wish. You're the only person, I feel, who can help me at this point. My husband is gone."

He tossed down a bill, saw in a wild edge of his eye that it was a five, and would have turned back for it, but for his state, her here, the boy coming their way, the—

"I'm sorry," he said, and breathed to give himself space to speak. "I have an obligation to attend to."

He walked off.

2

A*nd* out the door, displaced, into a muffling transformation that made the muted buildings around appear to be swaying as they gave up their substance, and which was, he saw, as he flinched against the freighted complications over his face, snow. Blurry flakes of it draped the breadth of the street in a dampening cottony fall that scarcely shifted (that lowered in trancelike sideslips), and the flashes of ruby lights at its base as the brakes of cars and cabs were worked were like pedal notes witnessing its whiteness to this city where the absence of color was so seldom seen. His indecision about turning east or west participated in its milling vastness.

"Poppa John!"

The voice sounded like Celia's. And then he saw her coming down the street, under a canopy, with a miniature shopping bag over an arm, and at that moment there was a catch in her step and she came up in a run and fell against him with the force of an uninstructed lover, knocking him back, attempting to make an embrace of it, laughing, and looked up. "Isn't it lovely!"

It was as if she'd described herself, luminous in the crystalline shift and fall, with her body adjusting its familiar curves to his, and the presence of her here now like this had him practically weeping.

"Your instincts are so right! They always are. It's become Christmas for me at last. I knew exactly where to go and what to get." She drew back, and her eyes went into him in deepening probes. "Oh, dear. It's your pop."

He tried to nod but in the furry foliation felt like a child who's been lost and numbly stoic up to the moment he's found. "Somewhat. Muh—muh—muh—" It was the stutter that could seize him off-stage, or in the aftermath of the face, and angered him with its flailing at the border of a point. He took her elbows and in a shuffling half-dance guided her backward and to the side through the snow-dimmed crowd, moving on legs that seemed of varying lengths while he remembered, once on the way to his psychiatrist, trying on a pair of shoes, or actually the right one, which the salesman prodded and rubbed and pinched for fit, and then leaving in a lumbering gait that grew worse as he went, as if that leg were lengthening, to which the psychiatrist said, "You're really suggestible, aren't you? Was it because you knew you were coming to see me?"

He got her to a NO PARKING sign beside the

canopy, where they were still within the distracting animation of the snow, and weaved on his feet. *Tent pole*. He was out of breath and the dance had left him with the sensation that they were whirling, slow as the flakes, at the edge of the blackly glistening street.

"Poppa John, you weren't drinking in there, were you?"

"Not a drop." Drink brought it on.

"You had to use the rest room. It's him, then."

"Somewhat. Much ameliorated by you. And other things. I realized how long it's been since I've been able to be alone and think." This had just now fully occurred to him. "It was different this time."

"Worse."

"Oh, no. Not so severe. Hardly a twinge."

"That's a relief."

"Indeed. The only reason it came is I haven't been at work as I should—"

"I understand! I've felt that, too, and felt like, well, like an albatross. I haven't been much help."

"I've decided to stop by the agency today, since I'm out." This, too, had just occurred to him, in his need not to interrupt her pleasure, and his words were merely words meant to free. "I'll see if our situation can't be eased."

"Why, that's a wonderful idea! When you think of the sums you've earned over the years, it seems the least that fellow could do. How practical of you!"

Her breath formed climbing clouds in the dense
flakes, and she blinked as if to clear her vision (she'd
been somewhere, he saw, to remove the stripes of
mascara), and then blinked hard, with such force
she had to swallow, as if pressing excitement back,
and he felt, for his lie, the sick slide of shame he
had on that Broadway curb.

"I can't wait till you see what I've got you,"
she said. "Or so far. I've had one thing in mind for
months. I'm toplessly excited."

She grabbed her lapels and lifted the fur coat
back on her shoulders, like an ingenue exposing her
wealth, and laughed.

He looked across the street, to avoid her eyes,
and saw a policeman on the opposite corner step
down from the curb to cross against the light and
then step back up on it, fretful, when the man beside him stayed.

He said, "It was necessary to get out to decide
something so simple."

"Your instincts, love."

"It seems, rather, that this is rock," he said, and
lifted a hand as if to knock on his head, and saw
again, with a new vividness in the snow, that the
hand was bare.

"Shall I come with you?"

"Oh, no. Wouldn't that look as if we were trying to apply some sort of pressure? I'd be ill at ease.
No, go on with your shopping."

"I have two more things to get, and then I wanted to have my hair trimmed." She shook its heaviness in the blue skein, which was catching snowflakes. "You should, too. Your mane is getting shaggy, brother bear." She leaned and nipped his arm through his coat; then grinned up at him. "Well, I can't kiss you in the street, can I? Your eyes are always bluer out of doors, but in weather like this they're positively faceted. I haven't seen them so in months. How I love you."

"I—" He looked around for a focus to the cavernous anxiousness spreading from him into the street, and kept encountering, like counterpoint to the dispersal his senses were in, the agitated distraction of the snow.

"It's so difficult to talk here, like this," he said. "We'll see one another soon."

"I understand." She touched his coat sleeve.

"Which way were you headed?" he asked.

"I was going south."

"North," he said.

She gave him a grip. "I love you."

"And I."

He walked off. The cold hugged his back again, in a pattering travel that made him feel it must be her stare, and he slogged along in his stride as well as he could. But he felt slowed and amorphous, like the snow, amoeba-like, yet with a heaviness of lead at his center that his weakening knees trembled to keep up. He crossed with the light, passing the policeman, but, once up on that curb and beyond the corner building, didn't feel safe. At least from her. He went on to Fifty-eighth, turned west toward the Fine Arts, and caved worse as he scoured the block for an anonymous restaurant.

He'd have to go back to Lex. The day he'd leaned against the building and cried out against his psychiatrist, she'd steered him into a Bickford's and bought him a bowl of milk, and then had broken crackers over it, as her mother used to, she said, while he watched her working-woman's hands snapping the squares and her bracelets slipping over her wrists above the steaming bowl; and it was the only thing that they, or the psychiatrist, after another year of visits, had been able to discover that was of any relief when he was emptied of his father like this. "If it works," the man said, "use it. With such a harmless ritual, what have you got to lose? You're going to have to learn to live with this somehow."

Of course, there was no money to see the man now.

He went into a place where everybody seemed to be leaving, as if because of him, and up to the counter and stood. His knees quaked. He felt a presence and turned to the plate-glass window, which was painted along its lower half, and saw the heads and upper torsos of people passing as if in procession, all of them in black hats and coats, or so it looked through the granulated drapings of the snow, and it was as if he were watching the future from inside the day of his real death. Their faces might be any, yet they looked like people who would settle into recognition, if he knew their ages, or what year this was. He felt the pressure on him would squeeze out a last droplet of urine if he moved, the mandrake drop. Then there was a bustling close behind and the breath of a scent like Jean Naté.

"Yes. Could I help you, sir."

He turned a bit, unable to look at her. "I'd like a bowl of hot milk and some crackers, please."

"There are seats, sir."

"I'll sit in a booth."

"That's somebody else's station. Er, section."

Not sure for the moment if he was able to sit, he eased himself onto a stool at the counter.

"I don't think we have that," she said, and plucked up a menu from the rack in front of him. "This cook here's a real prima donna. He isn't doing anybody any favors, that guy."

"He can heat a glass of milk in a pan. I'll pay. I'll make it worth his while, tell him."

"I'll see."

He raised his knees against the countertop to hold himself against a molecular surge whose grayness engulfed the restaurant.

"What's the sensation like?" the psychiatrist once asked.

Poppa John

"I feel my body is physically disintegrating and I have to hold on to my mind with all I've got or it'll go. Or explode."

"But it never does."

"Not yet. I'm hanging on!"

"The next time that happens, why don't you try to relax and follow where the feeling takes you. It can't be worse than what you expect."

"If I could describe properly how it felt, you wouldn't say 'relax.'"

"It's a fairly universal feeling in clinical anxiety. I know myself how painful it is. I bet you'd rather have a leg cut off at the knee."

A laugh choked from him at the aptness of this. "How true! That would be something I could deal with!" How did the man know himself?

"And you could pretty much chart the recovery, which you'd no doubt—ah, with some *loss*, of course—expect."

They both broke up. The man's low and breathy *heh heh heh* came from his center and had a salacious sound to it that his eyes conveyed, along with kindness—a stimulant to laughter.

"Heinrich Böll—I believe it's Böll—has a story about a guy who tied a foot to one arm and learned to function that way. Everybody commented on it, of course, but the guy got so good at it he joined a circus. People were paying to see him do these things they'd made fun of him for doing before. Then he decided to untie himself, and be the way he used to be. What do you think?"

"I think you're making it up."

"You know, when you're not using language to keep things at a distance, you have other devices. You're really blessed— I shouldn't use that term in conjunction with you, *Poppa John*." His stomach, like a separate entity below his chest, and with the belt across it (which Poppa John was fixed on), lifted and shook. "You can exercise tremendous charm. Of course, I never know for sure when you're *acting*."

" 'Open rebuke is better than secret love.' "

"You see? Is there anger under that? Or are you grabbing at the blanket again?"

"Grabbing at the blanket?" He was startled.

"I haven't told you this?"

"No."

"Oh, goodness." He leaned forward, with laced hands between his knees. "Our friends had a little boy who liked beer, from the time he was about two, so they always poured a little in his glass when they had some. Then they noticed the looks they were getting when they ate out, as if they were encouraging the kid to be an alcoholic. So they told him, 'From now on, when we're out at a restaurant, you have to drink soda pop.' So the next time they were out, they asked the kid what he wanted to drink, and he said, 'Beer.' They said, 'No, now, we've discussed this and told you that when we eat out you have to drink soda. Now, there's this and this and that kind of soda. Which kind do you want?' And the kid said, 'I want my blanket.' "

And then the waking dream that he'd been trying to gather at the sideboard this morning unraveled before him over its full course. He was in a basement (not the one where he'd tended the furnace) that seemed by its feel and smell to be brand-new, but it was too dark to make out surroundings in detail. He was watching the edge of a sheet of paper that kept rising jerkily up from a strip of clear plastic, like a plastic rule, as if this were a partial representation of a teletype, whose bulk seemed to tremble in the darkness beneath. But the paper was blank. There was silence around the phenomenon. Above, upstairs, there was a crowd, as there had been at his father's wake (too many to watch), which he'd left, to come down to the basement; the thumps of their feet overhead on a floor suspended low. And then a present sound of wailing that wasn't a part of the wake entered the silence, and he turned and saw that the far corner of the basement was lit. The light there was brilliant, yet he was seeing it through such darkness and shadow, past enormous overhead pipes and a shape to the left that might be, after all, a furnace, that it looked closer when he first turned than it was. Footsteps were coming in sandy scrapes down the concrete stairwell the light poured from, and the wailing voices grew as the footsteps neared.

And then Celia stepped into sight, carrying the limp and wobbling body of a baby in her arms, weeping with a grief he'd never seen in her, while a child like a daughter followed at her side, wailing out of a silvered face. And the dream-sorter in him went: *One of the twins.* And then in the smother of no air, as he tried to cry out *Whose fault was this?* he was struggling so badly he broke out of sleep.

It was with that that this had all begun.

There was a rattling beside him and a bowl of milk came down with a heated scent, and then a pile of packaged crackers on a plate. He fumbled out a pair of bills, dropped them on the counter, and went back to a booth and moved over against the wall, as he liked to be, and locked on the reflection of a salt shaker in a napkin dispenser, which he took, for a startled second, to be him. The frazzle of cellophane, and then his hands seemed hers, braceletless, breaking the crackers into the liquid beneath, package after package, until they were gone. He stirred and poked at them with his spoon, and then gobbled it all down so fast there wasn't time to wipe at the spills that came in a mazelike crawl through his stubble. It was as if he'd eaten the liquid that allows your innards to be observed in an X ray. He could tell that they existed, and from them warmth spread wide, until his outlines and then dimensions felt secure. He was a measurable entity; and his frame of mind, with the complications still contending beneath it, shifted into a milder key. He scrubbed at his face with a napkin, and belched.

"Pardon," he said.

Pardon, Poppa John? Celia would have said if she'd been there. "This is no time for manners. I realize how relieved you must feel."

Yet there was an uneasy tenderness, still, as of a splinter that couldn't be got at and was plumply decaying, and then he realized he didn't have a job.

He remembered the dazzle of the woman who came to their door after his father's wake. Her rounded hat was of fur and she wore a fur coat that shimmered with fresh flakes and hung open to reveal chains and necklaces draped in loops from her neck to her waist. She said, "I've brought you a parcel." She'd read about the "atrocity" in the newspaper, she said, and told them that she'd lost her own husband a few months ago, to an illness that had kept him lingering, so she knew how they must feel, at least partly, and sympathized. She seemed as at ease, given the situation, as if the flat were hers, and sat in a cobbled-together chair with a grace that her mourning look transformed to placid commonness. Sparkles of drops now clung where the flakes had been and had melted. She had five grown sons, she said, who would "take over the business" for her now. "Thus I find myself in a position quite hopeful, compared with yours."

The parcel contained fruit and candy and a hundred dollars in gold pieces, they discovered after she left. His mother went to her knees and looked out their window toward the emerging sun, as if to pray, and whispered, "She's far, far away and above lace-curtain Irish. She's a true *grande dame*." And then: "She's not well."

They were invited to Sunday dinner, to a place not far from Gramercy Park, where there were tiered chandeliers, a fire in every fireplace, and all five floors hers: a house. There was a balcony across one end of the main room, with stairways leading down from either side along the walls—turned posts and newels and rails of polished wood—and as he studied the marvel of this, Celia appeared from a door in a white dress, walked along the balcony, and started down one of the flights of stairs, with those striped stockings that were fashionable then blurring beneath with her hurried strides. The grown-up brothers turned for a moment from their chairs around the main fireplace, as if in approval, and then went back to their talk and drinks. That people like this drank, too! She came up and stood behind the couch where her mother was and appraised him with the noncommittal thoroughness of that age, as he did her, not wishing to appear to be examining, yet examining to the core. She was a year older, a league of difference at going-on-twelve, and female, besides. Way ahead. One brother mentioned the name of somebody, and another replied, "If he was good enough for Father, he's good enough for me!"

And she turned to them and said, "It seems to me that if you keep talking about how Father ran the business, pretty soon you won't be able to run it yourselves."

They looked at their mother, who appeared to have lost her composure at this, and then laughed and slapped one another's backs. It was time for dinner. There were servants in white gloves waiting table. He'd been prepared for such a possibility by his mother, and so had an idea of what to do.

They were invited over on the first Sunday of every month for the next four years, and then Celia's mother's illness confined her to bed. She died. By now he had quit school and was working for a greengrocer on the West Side; he loaded up vegetables on the docks and delivered them in a snuffling truck across the lower end of the city. Every time he passed Seventeenth, traveling on Second or Third, he craned his head around to see the house. Or Celia outside it. Never.

Then he was called to be an actor; there was no other way to put it, because there was no decision involved. One day he was. He and his mother had moved to a smaller place, off Tompkins Square, and she wouldn't allow him to live with her any longer,

she said, if he planned to ruin his youth in a profession she was set against. He took a room near
Prince, among the Chinese, and gave up his job. He
became understudy to an actor-director who was
the rage then, and realized the man expected him to
be a replica, and one day said, out of his temper and
years, "I'm not you, sir, and wouldn't care to be,"
and walked out. The man had influence in the
theater and blackened his name throughout the city.

He eventually had to give up the room and
live off the charity of friends, who became less
friendly, and then weren't. He slept in parks or
deserted buildings, sometimes waking with the
thought of his father lying in that factory never to
wake. Once he sat up in morning light in the rubble
of one and, in a sequence he could never retrace,
rose from the same spot at noon with rats scrabbling
clear and his nose and mouth running blood; apparently he'd passed out. He went to steal food from
the docks, but pride or scruples restrained him once
he got there. He cleaned himself up and went to the
house on Seventeenth.

A woman, Celia, answered the door. He was
about to ask for food, or a loan, even a dollar to
make it through the day, like any beggar, when she
asked him in. He talked about becoming an actor,
without, however, mentioning his troubles, and kept
glancing around for lunch, or even tea, to appear
on a cart and be served. The longer he put off asking,
the more impossible it became. She was too attentive

to him. He got up, smelling a meal beginning somewhere back in the house, and she said, "Just a moment. I have something for you."

It was a collected works of Shakespeare, bound in tooled leather soft as an eyelid. "It used to be Father's," she said. "No, take it. I'd like it to be used as it was, daily, and my brothers don't care. They won't know it's missing. Someday the city will toast your Hamlet as it did Booth's. But you'll be watched by even more eyes than he was, I feel that."

He riffled madly through the book a block away but found no money in it. He took a job with the greengrocer again, and it wasn't until five years later, at an open tryout which he cut work to go to, that he got his first paying job. In a while he was working with Otis Skinner, and then Barrymore, and, after Barrymore's 101 nights of Hamlet, knew that he'd never do the role. But he did, at last, in repertory, out of doors, in the Catskills, and after the last performance, among the meager messages and cards, mostly from members of the company to one another, there was a single carnation with a note: "You should bring this to New York and mount it with a cast worthy of you. Celia."

She'd come up to spend the summer at a local spa and had seen him in six performances. They sat at a table on the terrace of her hotel and talked as the night crowd thinned and drifted off. Her brothers were squabbling about the business, she said, which was metals manufacturing, and two of them, the two oldest, lived with their wives and families in the house now, so this was added to the predicament of the business, and hers, too. She was to oversee the house as a place to entertain, and felt she was mostly mopping up after those two.

He tried to cover his embarrassment at the seedy troupe she'd caught him in with drink and extravagant claims about his prospects. He was in a fog of shame, and worse, for weeks afterward, whenever the memory of his tongue, leaping leagues ahead of his accomplishments, overtook him as he walked (while, on the other hand, he couldn't remember if he'd told her he'd peddled her father's book for fifty cents, though there was a raw spot in him that suggested he had); but what was even worse, as he kept being dragged back to that table, with the summer night beyond vibrating with insects, was the look in her gray-blue eyes: they lay in level openness over him, moist with admiration, urging him on even more.

It was when he was in the city working with Welles that he felt he could inquire about her, and called the house on the telephone. She was there, but sounded distant and evasive, if not unwell. He invited her out to dinner, and learned that the troubles between her brothers, which she'd been trying to arbitrate as her mother might, had grown worse; two weren't talking to one another, the two who lived at home, and both seemed unreclaimable alcoholics. She was in tears. He asked her to marry him that night. Let me think, she said. Her brothers were opposed, of course, and had her sign a document that turned her dowry and inheritance over to them. This he learned later. For her, she said, it was a relief.

But then they kept her in the house, out of touch, trying to persuade her to marry into a family they'd been courting about a merger, to save the business, they said, and the family name; now they were united. She'd been pursued by two of the sons from that family, earlier, and was, indeed, in the case of one, more than interested. This, too, he didn't learn until later, after they were married. All he knew was that she never answered his messages and never came to the telephone. And when he did hear, at least partially, of her predicament from her, in whispers over that instrument one evening, he ran over to Seventeenth and shouldered open the wide front door.

All five brothers were in the main room, as if in conference, as they'd been once, looking old and stout, with their rogue's reddish faces and Punchinello chins, smiling like sharks.

The oldest of them grabbed up a poker and another slid a hand into his coat.

"What is the charge for breaking and entering?" one of them asked, in general.

"Celia!" he called up the stairs. "We're leaving!"

"I couldn't tell you, exactly," another said. "But

I do know one has the right to defend to the death his hearth and home."

"That's what I understood."

"Do you suppose we five could handle a copper's kid who's turned *th*issified actor?"

There was bristling laughter among them.

"Celia!"

She appeared with a purse and her coat and started down the curving stairs.

"How many witnesses to this?" one asked.

"She'd be away and wouldn't have seen it," the oldest said. "Or had to be put away long ago for this hysteria of hers. Recall that?"

"I'd say I could take on all five of you, from your looks," the cop's kid said, and the two who had started for him stopped in their tracks.

"This is our parents' house," she said, "and it's been home to each of us. They made it so. If I have to call on God himself! to impress on you their memories, and the lives they lived so we'd have such a home, I will! You'll receive payment in the mail for the latch. Take my arm, dear."

They turned their backs on them and walked out.

And now snow passed the upper part of the green-painted plate glass in the way that all passed and would pass over the years. The first melt of the first spring in your memory, when you were wearing something funny over your ears—the quality of the light, then, new-minted, across the brownish grass and melting ground, as though you might melt yourself, and the moment never leave, and then there came a day when you felt a bit older, and looked up to find yourself being treated like an old man. Which you were.

All five brothers dead now. Sons and grandsons guiding the business, going on its original momentum still, with yet more divisiveness. The house no longer in the family, which kept him and Celia in a wide steer of the street, so that he couldn't say whether 221, with its red-brick front, was still there. When this trend got to its lowest, as though down a rusting fire escape into an area at the worst end-stop of a subway run, all he had to do was remember her in her white dress, with the blur of her stockings beneath, coming down those stairs as if into his arms and bed, and the entire block as it existed was restored. He lived in agelessness again.

He hadn't told the interviewers about his fears of the media, which took different forms, though one of the worst was over the false sense of continuity implied. As if unspeakable change didn't everywhere and in all things almost daily occur. He'd told executives willing to listen that anybody who could see could see things giving way, the old going under, the country itself on its way to hell in a coal bucket, but as long as you could get in front of a set and enter into those images (which made you feel a fool if you didn't put off your guard, relax, and follow them through), it became difficult to believe that there was anything wrong to begin with.

Like an unpleasant show before the present one. After all, here came Poppa John, or that cowboy, or the newscaster you could trust, and your mind was skimming along in a dimension whose activity precluded any sealed-off thought. The continuity that used to be built into chores and family life and activities that involved you with others, along with examinations of whatever came up to interrupt that, from inside or out, got fuzzed over, and the lack of it was strung along the arbitrary schedule of this substitute. Once conditioned to it, you were gone. Those long hours of living inside its box.

It was what he was doing now, without a job. Ignoring the truth.

But its worst effect was on children; look at the twins. They'd grown up with it and had no idea of a creativity that was internal. They watched it from morning till night, a working day, or more, as other children must. How could they tell what was real on it, in their wavering between fantasy and the literal, when their parents got so involved? "It's only a program," their father said, but what did *program* mean to them, and could he explain how the scenes of the present war were different from other killings that appeared? Did it make any difference to them? Or him?

Poppa John had seen how a radio show, with disclaimers all the way through, had affected the entire East Coast, where intelligence and sophistication were supposed to abide, when Welles aired his production of the invasion from Mars. General hysteria. Parkways packed in snarl from the exodus. And it hadn't employed the additional vehicle of images, which moved and mirrored life's everyday aspects, without, however, conveying its complexity or physical limits. Instead of referring back to this, and considering the possible effects of an even more powerful medium on children, the executives let the fare every year become worse.

A new actor was added to the show near his end—one of those steady sorts who have a facility for appearing natural on camera, because they seem to be thinking everything painfully through, and often are. A good Horatio. Poppa John caught the fellow studying him in a covert way, and then he came up and asked if they could get together, "to talk about the structure of the basic people the action here is centered on, and maybe something about their past relationships with others, you know. If you have time. I admit I'm confused. You look like the only guy who knows what's going on."

He'd decided before this, since he knew by now he was leaving, that the least he could do was ease a few of these newcomers along. It might help him handle some of the self-pity which would eventually come, he felt, and he wanted to conduct himself, as much as he was able, as a professional. The art of the ambitious young, anyway, has always been to devour well-aged minds while wiping their mouths with awed innocence. And he felt sorry for the fellow; his wife was the lead in one of Broadway's longest-running shows. Her Tuscan looks, with those wide-set eyes that stared out with incendiary fervor, or from a horror about to be released, were being copied by magazine models and filtering down to the street, after a study of them via the magnification of movies, where she'd worked first.

He and Celia went for dinner. The actress met them at the door, so grave he understood at once that the smile which was seldom seen on-camera, and which he'd assumed she reserved for effect, was impossible to force, a part of her. She stepped back, in a clinging black evening gown, and let them in. A darkened vestibule with a mirror in a gilt rococo frame across from him. He kept glancing into this, to reassure himself of his turnout, due to the effect of her stare after a five-flight climb for their health, and realized, as she went about the business of getting their wraps, that the whitish portion of her gown he was seeing in the mirror was actually her back; it was bared to the waist and below. He wondered how she was trussed in such an outfit, and then, as she stooped to pick up a scarf she'd dropped (her hands were shaking), saw that she wasn't. She stepped past the mirror through a door, where the edge of a bulky bed wavered in candlelight, dropped their coats, and turned and tipped her head to arrange her hair in the dark shine of a window.

A hall led off to the kitchen, to judge from the aroma, and in a room to their right the purplish fluctuations over the single wall he could see signified a television set. Lowered Austrian shades gave a wrinkled, skinlike action to the shifting light. She led them in and up to the actor, who was slumped in a chair in front of the set, as in a spotlight, in a casual sweater of the sort he wore for his role, and he turned and said, "Hey, Poppa John, you made it. Great."

Celia mentioned how nice the room looked. In the bluish night-blindness that came with age, Poppa John could make out a row of ferns along the wall where the shades hung, some lumps of furniture, and squares up high that must be paintings, but kept being drawn back to the actress, as if to fathom the meaning of her look, which seemed to single him out. She asked if they wanted wine or cocktails and they both said, "Neither," uneasy, and went to a couch and sat. She turned to the television, as if drawn by her husband's attention, and then there was laughter from a chair in the corner. "Oh, girls," she said. "This is Poppa John and Celia. *He's* on TV." Then she turned to go down the hall, the flash of her back an illusion, it looked, if it weren't for her shoulder blades and moving spine and the curves at its base.

"Say, girls," Poppa John said. "Can I come over and say hi?"

They giggled, of that age, not quite in school, and then he noticed, first, the matching dresses. They were identical twins. He stood, surprised, and one said, "Oh, la Poppa Doppa," and the other, "Ooo Ooo," and both burst from the chair as he took a step. They peered from behind either side of its high back. The hair of both, as black as their mother's, clipped around their faces like fitting caps, made their fine features look even more fragile. It was their eyes, brimming with her burn, but not the knowledge that gave it depth, that held him, and then they were drawn back to the television, and their faces assumed the expressionless cast of taking it in.

He went down on a knee in front of the chair. "How old are you?"

This brought out a chattering, and then their laughter, which ran breathlessly down identical scales, and was cut off by a sway from the one on his left, with a missing tooth, who must be dominant.

"You girls be friendly to Poppa John," their father said from his chair. "Pretend he's your grandpa."

"Oh, Grampoppa Poppa," the one with the

missing tooth said, and seemed at the border of being frightened. "Wha' beeg mahn."

"Wha' beeg hahn to fuzz on he face," the other said. Or so he heard it.

"Cap'n Kangaroo!" they both chirped, and Poppa John suffered a pang; he'd often wondered how that Keeshan managed to do so well with children.

"Naw, naw, *Poppa John*," the voice from behind said. "On my show. Pretend he's your grandpa." And then, apparently to Celia, "They've only got one, you see, and they've only seen the old man a couple of times."

They slapped the back of the chair. "Set-te, Grampapoppa."

"Poppa John's twins," he said, and sensed he'd said too much. He sat and in a movement which seemed timed with his, in a whirl, their skirts went up, so as not to wrinkle them, and each was on a knee, leaning against his chest. He didn't know what to say, or if he dared move. He couldn't remember the last time he'd held a child, other than a child actor (most of whom were hardly children), and then his attention would have been beaming out to make an artwork of the situation; his access to the remote past was unimpaired, but recent years bulked and blurred, and a day's events or appointments could slip past: fireflies among the fixed and permanent stars.

Their profiles, like one of those prints that will

change into a birdbath or chalice, or some single shape, seemed finer seen close up—the bulged dome of forehead and fillip of nose and dished-in face—but for the protruding upper lip. Long, brushlike eyelashes flicked in unison over the shifting patina of television light that covered their eyes. The heat of them astonished him. They were hotter than the heating pad he used on his knees, turned up full, volatile with the pressing humid density of body heat; and when one of them moved, the other did, until the switching of their fannies over his thighs caused him to blush. A knee quaked. He'd never been quite so entrapped by circumstance; surely their father knew how this felt.

The fellow said, "Now, girls, watch how Ilya gets out of this one. I bet a muscle hardly moves in his face." A spy show of some sort. "Remember, it's only a program."

Poppa John was invaded by an intuitive wash, or wisp of insight, in which a group was gathering at a conference table, their coats still on, and hurrying into discussion about— But as he tried to close in to hear, the room where this was happening, which lay before him so that it seemed he could walk into it, went. Then he felt he'd been in some accident, whose scene retreated from him faster than his inner vision could travel, and that the mirror of his mind, which usually gave out infallible information on what it reflected, had been smashed.

Then the actor turned in his chair, and said,

"Say, once you get inside one of these people on a regular show, you know, like ours, and think with that guy's mind, relating to all the other people on it, you're always on. In a way. Isn't that right?"

The actress, who'd come into the room sometime in here, said it was time for dinner.

The girls jumped up and whirled at this, chattering something he couldn't catch, and then slowed, watching the TV as they went—a man was shot with a grappling hook that one of the spies had intended to use for climbing, and both went "Oooo!" —and Poppa John perceived the Austrian shades as the textured emptiness across him where the twins had just been. He felt cold. Celia was beside the actress, waiting, and asked the twins their names, but they broke into flight down the hall, singing something in the distance.

The actor got to his feet, still absorbed in the television, and Poppa John was reluctant to walk past him, for the intensity of his concentration, but then did. He and Celia started down the hall after the actress, pale wedge, and the actor said, "I'll be right there. It'll just be a minute. Have some wine."

The dining room was at the end of the hall, near the kitchen. They sat and the actress tried to make conversation about the soap her husband was hoping to become permanent on, as she conveyed it, and then poured wine. Celia asked about the twins, who were across from them at the table, where correct settings for six shone on linen in the dimmed light of an electric chandelier spread abroad on rayed lines like a representational sunburst. They were chanting something to the jingle of a commercial for soup. Their names were Belinda and Claris, the actress said. Poppa John heard other sounds above their noise, as of a cook in the kitchen, and then the resonance of something heavy on wheels, like a tea cart, coming down the hall.

The actor wheeled the television through the doorway and squatted behind it to plug it in. The twins clapped and cheered. An elderly woman, in a maid's gray dress with white collar and cuffs, and with black hair cleaved down the center and pulled into a roll, stood in the doorway with her hands at her waist.

"My mother," the actress said, and went into a rapid patois that seemed part Spanish, as if she were learning to speak it. He was sure he heard something about Poppa John, but the television set, meanwhile, was on again, though set low, and the actor was taking his place at the head of the table.

Her mother smiled—she had her daughter's teeth, and a dished-in face and flattened nose that looked simian, atavistic—and then clapped her hands like one of the twins, and cried, "Ooo, Señor Poppa John! Muy hombre! Muy hombre inna máquina de películas!"

He turned to the actress, whose face was

lowered, eyes on him from below her brow, and thought: *Puerto Rican.* And realized the thought had registered as if he'd spoken it aloud.

"Muy hombre inna programa wis him," the old woman said, giggling, and pointed to her son-in-law, and the actor stared at his plate with such a darkened look it was as if he'd bit and bloodied his tongue. He grabbed up his wine and drank it down.

Poppa John was familiar with the sort; if he could get by with it, he'd trip you during a curtain call, to make you look bad, at the least, if not injure you so he could take your part, believing, in his access of conceit, that he'd receive your same ovation, or a bigger one.

And then his wife, who was taking this all in, said with the untrammeled hauteur of a leading lady not about to let an occasion for the dramatic slip, "David is sometimes embarrassed by Mother. Well, not her so much any more, as her taste. She tends to like to watch the shows the twins watch. There's nothing for them to do when I'm away at work and David out on rounds—or, no, at work now with you—except watch TV. I'm afraid that's habitual here."

"Well, Poppa John, you see, I kind of consider this a part of my training. I watch every sort of show and watch every actor on them, and I'm getting so I can tell what kind of movements and expressions you can use in that small space, and which ones look the least bit false, especially in the daytime shows. I study every eyeblink."

Poppa John was willing to bet he did.

"And, you know, it doesn't make any difference how many times you watch those old soaps, there's always something to watch for and you always get a bit interested. Oh, I couldn't begin to tell you the half of it, but I see how people get involved in them. They're druggy. I'm building up a whole library of what not to do, besides what I learn from those freaks. It's something I figure I have to keep up on every day if I'm going to be as good as guys like you." He smiled for the first time that night.

Poppa John was weighing leaving, against Celia and the actress, when the twins started singing something about being hungry, and patting their hands in time on their plates.

"Oh, be quiet, you two," the actor said. "What were you told? Pay attention to the end now, so you can't pretend you missed it. Look."

A couple of years before this, Poppa John had read a story in *The New Yorker* by one of those Johns he could never keep straight, though it was one of the ones who wasn't Scots or Irish, about a family in a restaurant saying TV slogans to one another as they ate, and had seen it as hyperbole meant to carry symbolic overtones or "relevant social comment," but realized now that the fellow had been recording an actual situation. Or was prophetic. There was more going on at the table than he could assimilate, and then, from the glimpse of that conference turning into an accident, he recognized that something wasn't right about the twins. Which Celia must have sensed immediately. It wasn't as if they were retarded, but they didn't seem to take in what was in front of them, except as it gave off echoes of the TV, and he felt a responsible weight for all the years he'd worked on it, like an unliftable yoke, settle over his back.

"The girls are not autistic, as some think," the actress said. "Or at least one child psychologist has assured us that she's positive they're not. It's the time spent with Mother, partially, she feels, from the time they were born—they're not comfortable in either language, it seems—and maybe partially this addiction they've developed, with the help of their father, for TV."

Most of her talk appeared to flow over the actor, but this caught; he turned his chair, which he'd turned so he could see the set, to her. "We didn't even have one till two years ago!" he said, in a voice he seemed to regret losing control of. "When I felt it was necessary—"

"We've always had one," she said to Poppa John.

"Ah! you can't call that little *portable*—"

"And beyond that, it was a difficult birth," she said to them.

"Yeah, Teresa's real tiny, the doctor said. Real

difficult for one, much less twins, and we were down in Mexico then. I was on location for one of those crackpot Westerns. You couldn't get good food or good medical attention. Maybe the birth was too long. That little local hospital there, why, it reeked of—"

"And I found it necessary to try some peyote," she said, in her voice of studied elegance which now sounded like a cover for an accent.

"Hey!" the actor said.

"Peyote?" Poppa John asked.

"It's a natural form of acid."

"*Acid?*"

"LSD. An hallucinogen." The poised turn of her free hand above her wineglass at this.

"Well, great God, Terry, you didn't have to tell them that. I mean, you might as well go into our private lives down there, too."

"I'd rather not."

Her mother had been moving around the table in shadowy silence, and Poppa John realized that the smoke he saw rising was from food; dinner was served. A paella, beans, fried vegetables, and another wine the old woman was pouring into second glasses. She gave the twins a tincture of it in their water and they drank it off in unison, like their father, in one draft. Their movements speeded up, but appeared more synchronized with their chatter, as if they were moving into a climax of their own.

"They're tired," the actress said. "I feel guilty

for what I did before they were born, guilty for the way they are, and guilty for keeping them up like this, but not half as guilty as I'd feel if I locked them up in a back room."

She bit with her white teeth into a piece of chicken, drawing some skin between her lips as she stared, and Poppa John wondered if it wasn't wrong to speak this way with the twins there.

The old woman was standing behind the two, with her hands on their heads, as if to hold them down, grinning wildly at him. The food was exquisite, too much to take at the moment, and he was able to manage it only with the help of his wine, which got him upset looks from Celia. Then the twins were off their chairs and out the door toward the kitchen, with their grandmother following—all talking in a language that it seemed only they could understand.

"They must think it's time for their cartoons out there with her," the actor said. "They sure are confused tonight. They thought he was Captain Kangaroo." He laughed, mostly in Celia's direction.

The actress produced a wrinkled, twisted cigarette from somewhere and lit it, sending up a high flare that died quick.

"Hey!" the actor said. "That's enough, now, isn't it?"

She put her elbows on the table, drawing wisps of smoke into her narrow nostrils, and gave a nod at the rustling TV. "You have that." It appeared she had to swallow hard. "And you know very well they want to get off alone, where that 'tiny portable' is." She turned to Poppa John and leaned as far forward as she could, crushing her breasts into the table, and said, "You see, our high and mighty *adult* attitude ruins whatever little bit of pleasure it is they're able to get out of this lousy life."

Another waitress, perhaps the one who handled the section his booth was in, brought a glass of water, and he drank it down as if to relieve an interior leaking. The actress was referring to his righteous reek, of course, although he was so taken aback by the night it was one of the first times in years he hadn't been in character. The meal got worse as the actor continued to drink and turned surly, and they left before they'd properly finished. And then the poor fellow, who seemed shameless, or without a conscience, or memory, continued to come up to Poppa John as though nothing had happened, and pry him about his part, always on the set, where Poppa John didn't like to be disturbed. And then was released from the show, for reasons nobody could explain; somebody said the producers didn't like his chin in profile, which was as likely as anything with those two.

Weeks later there was a stir on the set that Poppa

Poppa John

John still felt he had backed away from, as if to keep
his distance as it neared, and once he heard the man's
name he knew it had to do with the twins, and reex-
perienced the wisps of that conference, the texture
of the Austrian shades after they'd leaped up, and
how he'd felt cold. They'd gone into the master bedroom, where their parents were in bed, climbed
up on the sill of an open window, joined hands and
thrown up their arms—it was at this moment that the
parents said they woke up and saw them—and
jumped. One of them struck the curb of a flower
bed in the courtyard and was killed. The other
landed, miraculously, on her, and broke most of
the bones along one entire side, but lived.

The next morning it was on the front page of
the tabloids, because of the actress. Poppa John didn't
care to speculate about the reasons. The grandmother
had also been home at the time. He took up his Bible.
Celia stayed in bed for the weekend. They'd never
had children of their own. Him. They sent flowers.
They didn't want to know for certain which had
lived, or to imagine how the relationship of the parents might be affected, or the weight on the one still
living. It seemed a curse.

And then he was in the neighborhood of their
apartment one afternoon, in an import shop in the
East Seventies, looking through the caviar, and put
down the jar in his hand, and thought, Why am I
doing this? He walked the two blocks to their build-

ing and, as he came up to its entrance, relived that night scene: the police and ambulance flashers raking the faces of the crowd that always gathers, spotlights on the side of the building, and then the actress coming out the door in her long coat, with the actor at her side, putting an arm around her, his head down, while flashbulbs erupted as if at a premiere. Poppa John stepped into the vestibule and rang their buzzer. There was an elevator, but he walked up as he and Celia had that other time, and at the turn of each half flight felt himself weaken. As he came up the last steps, his knees going, the door of the apartment opened, and the actress looked out. And it was impressed on him with horrible clarity how suddenly beauty can become a washerwoman in housewraps. She let the door slam as she ran to him, brother and sister in this, and he pressed her oily musky head against his chest as if to contain the explosiveness of her sobbing.

"The Lord has always loved children," he said, "whether we consider them innocent or not. 'Suffer the little children to come unto me,' he says, 'and forbid them not: for of such is the kingdom of God.' I can't begin to imagine what it would be like to lose one. We'll help you any way we can."

"Say something else!"

" 'Therefore are they before the throne of God, and serve him day and night in his temple: and he that sitteth on the throne shall dwell among them.

They shall hunger no more, neither thirst any more; neither shall the sun light on them, nor any heat.' "

"Yes, I feel they're both dead! You don't know what it's like to see her lying there!"

" 'For the Lamb which is in the midst of the throne shall feed them, and shall lead them unto living fountains of waters: and God shall wipe away all tears from their eyes.' No man can make such promises."

He visited another time, again to find the actor absent, and was ushered into the twin's room and left alone. The room was large and plain but somehow looked disordered. There was a slant along one side of the ceiling, as if steps ran above, and the light was faint. He sat in a rocker beside the oversized metal crib where she lay staring up at the ceiling, silent, hardly breathing—and then a flick of her eyelashes reassured him. There were casts, and cords running to an apparatus, but he couldn't bear to examine how they were related to the stillness of her body. He leaned and picked up a book off the floor, Dr. Seuss, and read it to her from cover to cover. Then he pulled out his pocket-sized New Testament and Psalms and read from that. There was no response until the verse, in Psalm 91, " 'He shall cover thee with his feathers, and under his wings shalt thou trust.' " She smiled and looked at him, and then turned back to the ceiling.

A few weeks later, when he was near the end of

his televised dying, a note came from the actress saying that they were moving back to L.A. At its
bottom she'd scratched with another pen, in a shaky
hand, "Mother says they saw something and believed
they could fly." He was so involved with his death,
the show and what he was up to, the interview and
its aftermath, that by the time he called, they were
gone. He never saw them again. He'd since read in
the newspapers about her separation from the actor,
and then the divorce, with never a mention of the
twin.

Oh, children, he thought, taking in the empty
stools and chairs of the near-deserted restaurant,
children, children, how many of you have I
offended? A tear tipped off an eyelash and ran into
his stubble where he'd wiped at the milk. Drops
struck over his other cheek and ran until his eyes
were blurred hemispheres of a system that would
soon sink. He pulled out some napkins and scrubbed.
He'd never be free of the yokelike heaviness that had
come over him that night at their table, and was tied
to his original misgivings about TV and his role itself, with even further ties running into the depths
of that deeper well of his father's death. A hollow
echo still.

In that respect, he was happy to be out of the
business.

He tossed a bill down on the table and walked
out.

Poppa John

*

And was surprised, again, by the snow, which was falling as heavily as before but now bent in billowy lines in a turbulence that was sweeping it east, out over the ocean, whose yellowish waves he could picture in silence taking it in. *Now I am alone*, came to him from *Hamlet*, in the voice that he'd used for that role, and he carried on the entire furious soliloquy of self-hate as he went in his walk toward Fifth, sniffling as if he'd caught a cold. He stopped at a store where a television set, among others in a window, seemed to be broadcasting the snow he stood in, and then stepped back toward the store's entrance, and saw himself appear on the screen, as he'd imagined he had a moment before. He saw the Vidicon camera set high up; the storm was indeed being broadcast. And now seemed to shift farther out in its reaches, as he stared at himself from his audience of one.

At Fifth, he paused, facing the wind, and then went the cold gray block down past Tiffany's, then turned back to it. He stopped at the first miniature display window, like a framed picture set into the stone, and then went on to the next, and on around the corner (all his day so far seemed at right angles), where the park, with its skeletons of trees shrouded in snow, spread its separate wilderness at his back. The Plaza fountain, furring with the accumulated fall, was barren of the specious dreams of romance it provoked. Another framed picture: necklaces, silver-backed accessories, a hairnet of spun gold.

What would she want? It was impossible to express feelings with an object. There were your own impressions about it, besides what was seen in it by the one it was for, and these never coincided, or affected the object. And when you looked back on the gifts that had been given to you over the years by others, the idea of trying to select something, now, out of all that lay around, which might recapture for another a measure of the joy that you'd once felt, was almost too much for him to endure. It only reaffirmed how surely those others were gone.

When you were young, you received—nothing more—and that lay behind this indecision about picking a gift, especially at Christmas. You sat undeserving as more was heaped in your lap than you'd got over the rest of the year, often in an hour, and from the first of memory, that was your experience. Later, you might print a card or wrap up on impulse something near at hand, and give that. But it didn't convey what you felt for the person, or what you felt while you'd put it together, and didn't relieve the weight the season began to bring down, which broke loose in too much activity, busyness, or hysterical joy, as if by this you could avoid the crush of gifts on their way.

Until it occurred to you that to extricate yourself you had to give somebody else exactly what they wished for. You'd see in them the response you were sure you remembered. And when you did, what you saw was that wishes weren't so simple (considerations of where and how it was got and what it cost and how to respond now entered in), and you understood that even if you could give a building like this with all that was in it, it might not be adequate, considering the person. It wasn't the kind of giving that was more blessed than receiving, and the second you understood this there was a worse turn: something in people resisted absolute love. With nothing attached. The giving of objects couldn't parallel or match the deeds of those you first remembered, or the ways in which they'd otherwise affected you, or how their relationships attended to your daily needs. Or that they, too, had changed, or were gone, while some of their physical gifts to you still looked out from your shelves.

So why turn and heap things on somebody else, and especially a child, or Celia, to begin the cycle over again? Once in it, you were caught. You might well do it to get even, all the way back to your beginnings, he thought, and in this chancy speculation it seemed he had his back against that wall of brick around from their railroad flat, and was pulling on his shoes. And then the picture before him—the velvet backing with its array of jewelry—swung inward, and he was staring through a pane of glass at an ashen-faced clerk in a pompadour who was as startled to see Poppa John as Poppa John was to see him. Like the teller, the clerk could be Poppa John's agent, and Poppa John was assailed by the city fear of being pursued.

He walked off west. This grim carnival the city could spring. *Once in it, you were caught.* If there was ever a time when you wished for money, Christmas was it. All his habits and tastes and fears kept pressing him outward, as if extruding him (if that fellow hadn't appeared, he'd seen a pretty pendant, though probably at $1,750) into the mold of the man he'd once been, and the only thing keeping him from that, at the present, was money. He sometimes felt that three-fifths of personality was money—an appalling thought he'd never have had if he hadn't been comfortable for years as far as money went, and now without it. Just for the relief, one might cash a bad check, not to say if you had to get hold of necessities.

So far, there weren't any major bills that remained unpaid, and they weren't lacking, not really. But they'd continued to contribute to a church, by mail, and to several charities, until only recently, and now there was a growing pile of letters on his desk exhorting him to be his generous self again. If they could take on the burden of his guilt about them, they'd break down the desk. He and Celia were "foster parents" to children overseas, for certain sums, and this month, if he didn't find work, they'd have to stop the payments. For months he'd been wanting to call L.A.

He'd have to give up his thirty-year membership in the Players Club.

There was a clopping behind and he stopped to watch a carriage with a canvas top, drawn by a team of seedy grays, come on yellow wheels down the center line of the street, between the rows of cars and cabs, with the driver—in a battered stovepipe hat, leaning forward on his seat, his arms crossed to warm his hands, the reins somewhere under him— cleaving the snow like a figurehead from a fantasy turning to solid truth. Poppa John had lived when these were the means of transportation in the city, and the emotions he usually felt when he saw one, or even horses, besides the solidarity they called up in him for this community and island, which had changed so little, really, over the years, and was his home, were pierced through by a residual rush of his father's face.

He stopped at Seventh Avenue and looked to the higher stand of buildings where his agency was. A friend once said to him that you always stare up at the window of the one you love, but you also stared up at the windows of those you didn't. He turned and went back east. He'd seen his agent a week ago, without telling Celia, and never intended to see him today. Or, rather, he'd seen the nephew

of the agent he'd been with for thirty years, at the
agency which had become one of the most respected
and powerful in the city. The boy had sat back behind
his uncle's desk, staring out of eyes that were set
too far back in his skull, his face all concave lines
and fixed in some sort of control that kept it in a
scowl, as if he'd got in too deep, or thought the
look might seem to minimize his power, and he'd
said, as usual, as if weary, "What is it, Ned?"

What, indeed? Poppa John once asked him
what area it was he'd studied in school, for his own
information and Celia's sake, and the boy's hairline
had altered as a dog bristles, and he said, at last, out
of a silence about to turn patronizing, "Ned, cut
the shit."

His mother, a society belle, owned a chain of
women's publications, and it was said that he'd
married into money. When people across the country
were watching the Last Days of Poppa John, Poppa
John's real agent, Russell, the boy's uncle, had got
up from this same desk in the middle of dictating a
letter, had gone to the window and leaned on his
air conditioner, "and then he was on the floor"—in
the shorthand his secretary used to convey it—dead
for real from a heart attack.

The boy could have had his uncle's money and
controlling shares in the agency and let an old
associate run it, and let it go at that, but chose to
run it himself. He'd just graduated from Yale in

some branch of journalism or English. He filled the
office with attractive young women, and for Poppa
John it was like walking into a preppy congregation.
Or libidinous finishing school. They all wore skirts
above their knees and gossiped about diets.

"He's busy now," one of them had said, when
he'd come in and started back to Russell's office out
of habit. He sat on a couch to wait; he'd always
walked right in. "If there's ever a time when you
wish for money, Christmas is it," was how he'd
planned to begin, and might have with Russell, if
he'd ever had to consider asking for an advance. A
young fellow he halfway recognized, with copper
hair parted up the middle and makeup on, so it
looked, and in a continentally tailored suit, came out
of the office smiling and waving at everyone, and
they seemed to cheer. What were trends for others
were for him, now, Poppa John had thought, para-
doxes. There were no enduring values in the styles
of life he saw emerging, as there was no warmth in
the clothes. The resistant vacuum of piled-on years,
though the same person, there from the first, resides
beneath. The train pulls away and leaves you on
the platform. A new engineer. A new—

"Sir," the girl was saying. "*Sir.* You may go
in now."

The boy was behind the big desk, with a drawer
pulled out and one foot up in it, leaning back in a
swivel chair, doing something to a paper clip as he
stared out of his ghostly, deep-set eyes. Poppa John

felt a swerve toward obsequiousness, which he sat on as firmly as he sat in the chair; the boy appalled him.

"What is it, Ned?" That weary voice dug.

"Well, if there's— I was wondering if there have been any calls for me."

"I'd let you know."

"I mean, any you might feel weren't important enough to call about."

"You'll have to give up the idea of daytime television, at least for a while, you know that."

"I realize I'm too popular for the general crew." He smiled; the scowl stayed fixed. "I didn't mean that. In television, that is. I meant something in a current show, say, or even something off-Broadway, that might be casting. Even a general call."

"Nothing that I've heard of for you."

"In any of my innumerable manifestations?"

"No, Ned."

"What about the mileage they continue to get out of yours truly on that soap? I heard myself mentioned twice in one segment last week. It's depressing. It doesn't help my standing much. Couldn't we say we wanted residuals on such mention, to put the throttle on them? One of those jokers is doing my wave like he inherited it. My memory is kept too green." He'd fallen into the role of the huckster he imagined the boy to be.

"That's something you and Uncle Russ should have worked out when you knew you were leaving,

Ned. I imagine you're too proud to apply for unemployment."

If he still smoked, here is where he would have
had one; two of him stared up from his best brogans'
shine. "Anyone who thinks unemployment is owed
to him, or free, can have my share." It had come out
nearly as he would have liked; he looked up. "I believe that you pay somehow for everything you get.
I'd rather work."

"But you've paid into the fund."

"I consider that a contribution, or necessary
dues, if you will."

"You're only hurting yourself, you realize, by
being so stubborn."

Poppa John glanced around the room; at a wall,
once a bulletin board layered with pictures and clippings and playbills, now bare; the windows looking
out over the roofs of buildings, which, from this
vantage, seemed dry empty pools; the air conditioner.
"Surely something must have come across your desk
in voice-over, say, that you could work me into."

"Ned, it's your voice, too."

Except for his fingertips, the boy hadn't moved
since Poppa John had come into the room, and there
was a coldness to this mention of his voice that sent
icy branches wagging close. Poppa John had audi-
tioned at the studios of a producer of commercials a
month ago, and everybody there—executives in
Hollywood corduroys and checks, young fellows in
blue jeans, men with the open-collar look of sound

engineers—had come out of the offices and studios and greeted him, saying, "It's you," and jokingly, "You really exist!" and then he'd sat at a microphone with the script and put on his glasses, taking in the suggestions for different approaches to the commercial, while being "natural," along with the import of what they wanted him to convey. But the moment he started to speak there was uneasiness; they turned blank and subdued, and as he was putting on his coat and beret drew back from him, with lowered eyes and evasive looks, and it wasn't until he was outside in the cold fall air, with the branches of the tree set into the sidewalk beside their carriage house nodding as if in affirmation near his eyes, that it came to him: they were offended that he was still alive.

"I've done classical work, you know, and I can do such a gamut of characters, if given the chance, I can't understand why that should be a problem. Or why I'm stuck by others in the same mold. Russell got me such jobs right and left when I was at the height of my popularity, as you might call it. Why, he—"

"Ned, you've become an institution. Maybe you overdid yourself."

This could be.

"People want to remember you as you were," the boy said.

"This is what I'm saying. That was only an nth of me."

"What about movies?"

"I'd rather stay in the city and get onstage. This is home."

"There are production companies in the city now."

Now? *Again,* Poppa John wanted to say. "But with nothing for me."

"Not at the moment. How about some ads? The cameo sort of thing where you're partly endorsing, you know, playing off your reputation."

"Selling stained-glass windows?"

This at last seemed to get to him. "Well, it would have to be the right product, wouldn't it? How are you at reading cold?"

"I can read a matchbook cover so you'd think it was life-and-death dialogue."

The boy tugged open the top drawer of the desk, pawed around, and tossed out a miniature matchbox. "Well, there's this."

Poppa John picked it up. "I suppose that was somewhat of a figure of speech. However." Holding it at arm's length, he saw only the name of a restaurant and *Made in Spain.* "Rather tight dialogue."

"Ned, you're at retirement age, anyway. Sixty-seven, or so."

"An actor, an artist, doesn't retire!"

The matchbox went bouncing back over the desk and even the boy, for an instant, was surprised; his scowl went and his eyes drew in on an area in him that was unexplored. And then he melted, or would have, if Poppa John's feelings for him could have focused. He'd had terrible suspicions that the boy didn't really look for work for him, and, after this, worse; that he might be saying he'd retired. He would have gone to a new agency that day, if it weren't that everybody in the business knew he was here, and had been for years. He didn't like to disrupt old relationships, and now that he needed work so badly, he was afraid that anybody calling in, and hearing he'd moved, would pause; and in that pause, in his present tenuous celebrity, write him off.

And yet he couldn't picture himself walking into that office again.

He felt he was striding out of his coat, and resumed the pace he'd take with Celia there. And then was stormed by the presence of a part-buried place. The New Hampshire manse. The few pieces of furniture, burnished with oil, their surfaces clear. The wood floor with worn but clean rugs and runners over it, the lack of decoration (a table cover with tassels that the Bible lay on) or pictures, even, except for a print like Doré of one of the prophets at the head of the stairs. A bookcase in the side bedroom—the room he slept in, on a cot alongside the desk, during their visits here—the books themselves invisible, but for the stampings on their backs, through the open door.

The living room at night with a pine tree, undecorated except for candles, in the corner; a bucket of sand near. The close space lit by the candles' flutter and (from the table with the tasseled cover) the rose-gold of a kerosene lamp—light that renders the walls insubstantial, hovering edges on the night banked over the house and village and surrounding mountains like fathomless snow.

On the floor in front of his grandfather's chair, staring up at the bronzed and shaved planes of his face; the big nostrils (one round, one tear-drop shaped) in his huge hooked nose; the glasses, of silver wire, with reflections that hide the eyes Ned can never anyway look into all the way to their depths; unlike his mother's—now on him from across the room—which disperse him over their surfaces.

"Open it, Grampop."

"Oh." A voice gone hollow. This is the winter he's failed, from a stroke or an accident; a fall from a stroke.

"Open it."

His mother makes signs for him to be more mannerly and patient. But he's picked out the gift (not the one she settled on, but what it was to be) and he's distributed it and the few others that were beneath the tree, under a sprinkling of needles, to the people they were addressed to, courteously, without opening any of his own, yet, and now this. The fragrance of the tree, increased by the heat of the stove, presses in on him in its bitter pungency, wild in this place, and makes the faces around (Grammom in her rocker) look more varied and expressive in the shuddering light; preserves their talk or laughter after it's stopped, as if lengthening it into the meditative quiet that seems to emanate from the head above and unite them; but also chafes at his impatience. "Open it!"

"Yes."

The old man revolves the tiny package in his knotty fingers and they tremble over the tissue as if sounding out its wrinkles and folds. "Yes, I feel." His caved-in cheeks, weathered and lined, hollow his voice even more and, affected by the festive atmosphere, take on the texture of the raised doughnuts warming in a bowl beside the stove. This is a barrel on its side, painted silver, a door at its end, that glows orange along its bottom while logs inside explode with the compact reports of the sound that's taboo.

The knotty fingers pluck at the colored twine, pluck and then pluck again and pause, relaxing in his lap, until Ned goes to him and unties the bow. His mother fastens him with a frown, but Grammom murmurs, "Oh, well, I'm afraid he's being awfully slow this year, Ruth, love, expecially for a youngster so keyed up."

She rocks.

"Here." His grandfather hands it to him and

he unwraps the tissue so fast he's scolded for tearing it beyond being reused, and pulls the object, a
pocketknife, out.

"Oh," the old man says, as a beginning smile
draws his bright brown lips downward. "Oh, yes.
That's fine."

"It's a jackknife, Grampop!"

"Yes. It's very fine. Wonderful."

"Look, Grampop, it's got all these geegaws on
it." He pulls out the blades, an awl, a leather needle,
a corkscrew, and closes them up; he hands it back.

"Oh, yes." Slim approval. "A fine knife. I've
had . . . I've seen . . ." Tears glide down gold from
under his glasses.

"Pop, it's nearly like the one you used to have."

"Yes, dear," Grammom says. "The one you lost
in the woods when you fell and had to be taken to
the hospital."

"The one you carried on the Oregon Trail, Pop.
Remember?"

"Oh, yes. The Oregon Trail."

"You were seventeen then, Pop."

"I was seventeen and . . . And I walked the
Oregon Trail. No horse or oxen. This knife was
all I had."

"Yes! Wonderful! It was your— It was
Neddy's idea. And would you believe it, Ma, somebody said it was bad luck to give a knife."

"Luck!" The right voice has appeared in one

of the transformations that can come so quick it's as if another person has stepped into him. "There's no such ingredient! Superstition shows a mind stuck in ritual, instead of lifted up in real belief. 'The lot is cast into the lap; but the whole disposing thereof is of the Lord.' God is sovereign." He looks down and says, "Thank you for your thoughtfulness, Grandson. You're a dear ornament to us. This season's celebrations are mostly pagan, but it's always a time to give."

He was standing outside Bloomingdale's, as removed from his sphere as a countrified tourist or half-baked actor goofing on drugs. In the crowd traveling past he saw a man with what looked like a plastic ear, waxy-white. He hurried inside, into a din confined. His eyes strained, pulled out of kilter by the memory, and difficult to get to focus, as if his sockets were sweating around them. At seventeen his grandfather read a part of Parkman's *Oregon Trail* and walked off the family farm near Higganum, so Ned's mother's story went, in order to see the West Parkman described, and came back seven years later, ordained and married, and was met at the end of the lane by his father.

"If you've fashioned your life without being accountable to me," his father said, "then live it." He'd wanted him to be a lawyer. He struck him from his will and added a codicil forbidding him to take part in the funeral or burial service. The prodigal son kept going to his father to explain and make amends, but the old man wouldn't hear him. And on the day of the funeral, the son sat under the lych-gate at the entrance to the country cemetery, in his wedding suit, with his daughter in his lap, until they heard the thumping of the dirt over the coffin, and then set her down and drew out his bandanna. "No reprieve," he whispered. "Forgive him, Lord. I scarcely can."

"Such is the family of man," Ned's pop would say, every time he heard this. "Such, my dear, is the family of man."

A manikin at a counter, apparently modeled on the young man who'd breezed out of the office of his agent the other day, swiveled to him, and said, "Yes, sir."

Surely a Christmas novelty, or addition, as at the bank. There was another nearly like it at the next counter, and the next, and . . . "Yes, *sir*." The sidling step and smile seemed artfully reproduced; another did the same. "Is there something I could help you with." A smell of breath under the cologne. They were real.

He was in the street, his head going in the two directions it does for a bar. There was a grayish one down a ways, with a canopy outlined in neon, and the need to be in it bore him there, it felt, while the

eyes of passing people pulled his features awry as he
strode. The place was packed four deep. Hoopla
music on a machine that sent pinpoints of light diving
in parabolas across the plastic veneer of its face.
Those near the door and standing farther back were
waving bigger bills. He tried to work his way up,
leaning low and saying "Excuse me" in an old man's
voice, as if he had to go to the bathroom. But there
was no mercy among them; hips and elbows locked.
Black hands opened a wallet next to his chest and he
saw a twenty extracted from a springy padding of
bills. Where did he— Where did people get that
sort of money? If desire could attract it, the walletful
would be plastered over Poppa John's forehead.

That and the rest of the waving bills he stared
wildly around at. Where did these people get it?
And how was it they all seemed to have so much?

His right hand and then his whole arm stiffened
and started to shake. He gave himself up to the
swells of movement until he was pressed against the
bar. The bartender nearest him, who hadn't shaved
carefully under his nose, seemed to groan in pain as
he shook something in a shaker close to his face, his
eyes closed, his short red jacket jerking above his
belt, and then poured twice, dripping and spilling
between the glasses as he swayed. Poppa John licked
his lips and, at home, if he'd been able to keep liquor
there still, would have sucked it off the bar.

"Double vodka on the rocks!" he cried, when

the man's eyes, not the man himself, appeared to tend in his direction. His legs grew thick, pumped up with impatience, and he planted them over an emptying trough it felt gravity would suck his sanity into, at his limit, about to create a scene, when his drink came in a plastic airport glass with the cash-register tape stuck to it.

He had to pay before he could even peck a sip; the man's fingers remained around its base. $2.52, he saw. No, he thought, as he slapped over his coat, and then tossed down a twenty that caused him to gag; no, it cost more than that. Satan calculated and kept exact tabs; the power of desire, as related to actual need, within the moment of the act. Esau selling his birthright for a bowl of beans. *For ye are bought with a price: therefore glorify God in your body, and in your spirit, which are God's.* It cost more than I have on me now, he thought, or more than Celia and I—

No, he thought, and stamped a quivering leg; it didn't cost a cent of her money. That's *hers.* He flinched at a burst of light in the back mirror that seemed to have just missed his head. He tossed down a two-dollar tip. The drink was gone. The last of it was going in a crawling sear down his esophagus, and then it struck his stomach with the breath-stopping burn of eating at the membrane over an ulcer. He gripped the bar and wouldn't budge in spite of the elbowing at his back and sides (feathers

over his intent) and then the pained-looking bartender with bristles under his nose pointed a finger
at him.

"The same!"

The noise and light seemed to speed up, yet veer
degrees away into a dampened zone, after he tossed
off the second. He'd go to the Village, where every
other person was an anomaly, or trembled at the edge
of the otherwordly from self-absorption, where he'd
grown up and was on home ground (he had another;
the man was on to him now, at two bucks a throw),
and shop there.

The divided rootlessness, after that, of being in
the street again, cold volumes and slabs of air over
his eyes. A slithering of icier flakes past his anes-
thetized state, as if caused by it. Which put people
and buildings at a double remove, and then his
walk itself, but charged the air across his face.
His breathing sounded magnified, moving among
echoing chambers in a draw of release and loss that
kept coming up as a pain under his ribs; the swaying
faces on the subway car. All their attention aimed
at him hugging the pole, aiming his own down at
the floor (a splash of incontinence on its tracked
and grayish tilt?), which a pressure behind his eyes
mercifully blurred, narrowing him in on the vodka's
numbing fumes.

Poppa John

Its fragmenting melt made random lights go up and down on isolated areas inside his mind and out, while the ringing iron wheels in their roll underneath said, over and over, *Please feel free to have the freedom to do whatever in your life you feel you must of necessity do to remain free* . . . Screams of curves and brakes he scarcely heard any more, his adjustments always seconds off, to the stop at West Fourth, where he and everybody in the car got off, it looked, and he had to give an autograph, a loopy scrawl that went flying outside its usual bounds, while a Jewish vendor of pretzels was saying to a crony beside him, "Boy, did I rook him on that."

Outside, the snow had stopped.

And then, in the first shop he went into, on MacDougal, a young woman, a girl, really, all in yellow, who seemed risen from a recent bath, a replication of Celia young, to the mouth and yellow hair, came up to him. She told him her size and showed him a suit on sale, a rust-colored tweed that she liked, she said, especially with the fashionable pants, and he held up a finger and said, "I'll take one!"

"Say, aren't you—" He did his wave and she cried "Too much!" and hugged him to the yellow in a bosomy crush; then looked up out of dewy gray-blue eyes. "I miss you on the show. Are you ever coming back?"

"Actually," he said as Poppa John, "I'm always

there"—he let his mouth tread around this in a masterful way—"in *spirit*, my dear. The necrophiliacs won't let me go."

She caught a whiff of the vodka and was drawn up into the intoxication that elevated in him at her touch. He saw a brownish sweater and put it down with the suit. He picked out a broad-brimmed hat, black, modeled by her, to replace the cloche, and got that. He'd picked up a multicolored scarf along the way. "Another sweater," he said, out of breath.

"Yellow or white?" she asked.

White. To keep this exchange separate. She boxed and wrapped it all, smiling and shaking her head so that her hair struck at her face as she worked, and then had him choose ribboned bows for each box; she stuck them on, and got it all into a big shopping bag, drawing a strand of hair from her lips. "Merry Christmas," she said, affronting him with her open stare. He waved and blew kisses as he went, crying "Merry Christmas" in his roundest Falstaffian tones, and then, outside, was assaulted by a group of those parapsychic panhandlers that the lower part of the city seems to breed. They closed in on him like crows around a carcass battered flat. He passed out bills from his pocket as he glanced up and down for a bar.

"Poppa John!"

The girl was coming out of the store with one arm out, trying to pull on a coat, bulky and blue, over the yellow, and got mostly into it as she came running up. And as she came, the street at her back seemed to widen into a lengthening vista, as if he were seeing at last, as he often felt, an entirely other existence in progress behind him. Then he realized (although a moment before it had appeared to him to be dark) that the sun was out, highlighting the colors up and down the bedraggled street; that the snow had stopped.

"Come for a drink with me, will you, please?" she said. "I'll buy."

"Oh, no. No, I couldn't allow you—"

"Please! I just walked off my job for you."

"You quit?"

"Oh, they'll have me back. I'm semi-invaluable. It's seasonal work. I'm a dancer." She did a Jacobean-like step and smiled, and her lips, seen in natural light, were fleshier than Celia's, and her even, squarish teeth, with spaces between and an expanse of gum above, were a child's. And now her nose looked larger and her hair bleached or dyed, and in this array of miscalculations he slipped into a blunter groove, and saw her as shorter, stunted. Which began fears in him about whether the suit for Celia would fit. And then she repositioned her legs under the coat and was at her real height.

"Hey, come on," she said, and took his free arm. "I know a great place. I was positive you wouldn't be like that old fogey you play on the tube. I practically had a bet on it. I could see that old light in your eyes." She gripped him tight. "You're so *human* right next to you like this. God, you're tall."

She led him around the corner to Sullivan, chattering about a summer company she'd worked with in Lommy Dew, Minnesota—"*L'homme Dieu*, but that's how they actually pronounced it, can you imagine?"—to a place with a neon sign that seemed to say "Goggles." Inside, she took him to a dark space across from the bar, where they had to squeeze between two round tables, whose tops were carved with initials and burnished orange from a jukebox bulking close, to get to a bench to sit. There was just enough sawdust scattered over the floor so that it might be about to be swept, or might be, as they said, for atmosphere.

"What do you want?" she asked, and rose, and from where he sat she rose into a shadowy stipple (an aftereffect of the snow?) that deepened in layers of darkness.

"Nonsense. No service?" He started up himself. "I'll—"

Her hands, large and strong, came over his shoulders. "No, sit. You're already sitting."

"Thus far, this much I've discerned." He saw a pair of bearded men at the bar with steins. "I'll have a beer."

"That's what I drink. How convivial of you!"

"Convivial? If I could carry along a tank of pure spirits, and have it tapped directly into my brain, I'd be more so, I can assure you."

"Oh, you clown! I thought I noticed you"— she pulled a hand out of a pocket and held it flat, the ends of her fingers curling up, and planed it around in the air—"wobbling with a wobble as you walked."

"My knees, they tell me. I lurch when led."

"You're loaded."

"I've had my holiday punch. Which I mean in the alcoholic sense."

She took in a breath that broadened her, bringing up her breasts, and from her look was about to smile. "Great," she said, and let the breath and moment go. "I'll get us a beer."

He crawled over a bit on the bench in the darkness and craned around to see a rest room. And realized his head was nodding down, as if dowsing over a liquid source. He leaned back and cracked the wall. The bartender, a craven-looking lout, was apparently saying to her in an oily Bronx accent, without moving his lips, "Mahsha, ya come in heeh with a ole faht like him, an expec me ta baleeve ya not a whooah?"

She came back with the beers, beaming, set them down, sat and opened her coat, and dropped it behind her like a discard as she leaned in. "There's something I want to ask you."

He grabbed his stein, as if to keep it from her,

and with the first swallow of beer the vodka in his
stomach rebelled with a convulsion that squeezed
tears into his eyes. He managed to keep it down
and say through clenched teeth, as he began to try
to rise, "I'm going to have to have something
stronger, I'm—" She reached and held him down
and the beer plunged up into his mouth in a spasm.
He saved it from flying by easing up a belch and
slipping the frothy slime down after, and this settled
into his stomach like a washrag over boiling fat.
She was at the bar and he believed he nodded
when a bottle of vodka was displayed. His ulcer
sent up a balloon that emerged as another belch.
He held himself still and kept swallowing against
the muscular constrictions that could cause him to
go into the bends of an utter heave. She set down a
vodka on the rocks.

And leaned in again, dipping to sip from her
stein as she stared with that affronting openness that
let him see down to her toes. "Actually, it's a favor.
I have a roommate who practically worships you."

"That's idolatry."

"Oh, don't be that poker-backed prude. She
thinks you're the best ever, on the tube, movies,
anywhere, and she works for a show like yours."

"The competition."

"She's behind the scenes, believe me. I don't
know how much she even understands about acting.
She thinks you're straight. I think you're a tremen-

dous actor. That's why *I* think you're great. I mean, you have to be able to act if you dance. You have to act with your whole body. I've been in two specials on NET. You're truly superb. She's still depressed that you died. She's not feeling well now. When I saw you, I thought what a gas it'd be if you'd walk in on her and wish her a Merry Christmas! She might unfreeze."

"It's the sort of thing I don't do as a rule."

She slapped his shoulder. "Stop being that old fruit!"

"It nearly comes under the category of a personal appearance."

"You need some bucks?"

He must have blushed at this. He swigged most of the vodka down.

"Come on," she said. "We live just up the street."

He stood, and saw the bartender wipe his nose with a thumb. "The rest room."

"Over behind the jukebox. One for all."

A stool in a black-enameled stall, a cube less than a closet, stinking of urgency and the cakes of scent placed over the tank top, down in a corner, over a sink with one faucet, besides the usual in its sausagelike shape gripping the bowl, down which a greasy black streak swung like a pointer to where everything went. The splattering thunderation of relief, and then a fiery closing pinch, like a red-hot

garrote popped tight at the base of it, making him
bite down on a cry; his prostate, lately out of synch.
He put it away for another place, and then went
out into the inky light and rocked above her. And
had to set a foot to one side, seeing her slip on a bias
and go watery, just as she looked up, with embarrassment, from finishing his beer, hers gone.

"Let's go," he said.

"You're coming with me?"

"I'll wish your friend a Merry Christmas."

Likely story, a clicking at the bar seemed to say.

"Don't forget your bag," she said, treading a
tight line of solemnity, and brought it up from the
floor.

The apartment was on Thompson, down a
block, five flights up. The five flights of everybody
he visited. He stood panting while she listened (her
eyes searching him as if he held the secret) at a
reddish metal door, receiving wallops to his heart
that opened his head onto a blackness where bits of
light went fleeing off like the last of consciousness.
He shook the interstellar absence into orbit, and then,
quick, down to size. His heart hurt. Or the lung
above it. He overheard his voice, in a line from a
show, say, *Never get involved with the young*. She
put a finger to her lips, took out keys, unlocked the
door, and her hands ushered him in.

The suggestiveness of a foreign place in its hush, unseen. Then a pair of studio couches, across from him, edged up, first, into his faulty vision. She came past on tiptoes and the door closed with a clong. It was a half-floor through, from what he could see, with a kitchen and perhaps a bathroom to the left behind a partition that didn't reach to the high ceiling. There were bare studs above (a flash of the powder room before it was finished), and the rest of the place was wide open, like a studio, with high windows along the wall beyond the partition. A table at his side, some boxes behind it, the couches there across from him, lengthwise against the wall, with a glinting cabinet between them, and some tinselly strands strung from above; that was it.

"She must not be back yet," she said, and walked in relaxed-at-home strides to the cabinet between the couches, slapping a loop of tinsel aside, and went down in front of it. "I'll put on some music."

"Something stroboscopic," he said, and heard the echo of Poppa John in the bare room. It felt colder than outside.

"Sit down," she said, with her back to him, and put a hand on a couch and patted it.

He removed his beret and felt so off-balance with the grip of it gone, he had to shuffle for footing; he pulled it back on; he stood where he was.

"She's usually back at two or two-thirty. It must be later than that. Do you have the time?" She turned to him from where she sat on her heels, and his eyes, to keep from the temptation, looked into hers, which now appeared violet.

He checked. He checked again. "Ten after three."

"Come here and put your bag down. You look like one of those old bag ladies, so lost."

A sudden chorus came from all corners, crying "Ba *bah!* dubba dubba dubba dubbadubba dubba"— this to Bach's *Art of Fugue*—"a dubba dubba dubba dubbadubba dubba da dee. *Bah, wah!*"

It was impossible to talk, or anything else, in the syllabic babel that severed his head. His sinuses were stuffed with the noise, and now other voices joined in at a higher level and seemed to press out white-gold wires that glowed along the junctures of the ceiling and walls. He sat on the couch, which gave and gave off emanations of a bed, and she rose and kicked free her shoes, and then slipped off her coat and dropped it on the other couch, turned and gripped something at her waist and, with the nonchalance of a cook at the end of a shift, was out of the skirt (which hit the coat) in a yellow body stocking. She went in a run toward the other end of the room, her arms rising, and leaped up on what looked like a bass drum lying on its side and went catapulting up into an end-over-end gainer, her feet appearing to brush the ceiling as her rigid body reversed in the air while she revolved, her hair raying out and then snapping down as she landed on her feet beside the thing, facing him, her arms out. And then raised up to her stretched height on her toes, as if being lifted by her winglike *port de bras*, and then was laughing, perhaps at him, from her looks, and he felt a riptide of loss.

Then the voices recapitulated the theme.

Her arms and legs picked up the music, but moved beneath it at a slower pace, and she appeared to step through rings and over the shapes of structure Bach had laid in place centuries ago, as the voices opened to allow Bach's line to come traveling from that day of its creation to this room, a fit place for it to be reconstructed, with the three windows letting in lengths of light that surrounded her in separate penumbras, and this seemed the meaning that her limbs in their movements were being used to trace, and this was the reason that she'd brought him here, he thought, and then with a leap she struck the trampoline again, and appeared to be doing a reverse, an unwinding of what she'd performed before, and at the peak of it, where her body seemed to hold against gravity and the mechanics of such a feat, there was a catch in him that rendered him blind and he saw the twins in their tumbling fall.

He rose and reached out, unseeing.

She was next to him, saying, "No, no"—he heard that much—and the voices came down in volume and left a pulsing vacancy that his senses strove outward to fill.

"And see if I can stir up some real Christmas cheer," she said. He heard that.

"That would be nice, please."

She was through the partition across the way, and in the void which had begun with her first turn and fall, sudden splintered spears of broken drunken thought—of the twin in her crib, the stab of her look; Celia's eyes in the flickery animation of the snow, and the years he looked back into looking into them, to his father's silhouette leaning closer to say, "Now, Sean, this Indian-boy detective"—entered his altered vision and revolved against the windows furled with sparks.

Then his mother's face, worn as it was at the last, was there. She'd died in a Village apartment, bare as this, but with newspapers piled along every wall, of pneumonia, the year he and Celia were married, and he'd sat in a rocker beside her bed, trying to rock regular rhythm into her breathing, and heard her breathe her drowning last. She wouldn't go to a hospital. She associated hospitals with the police. She didn't trust the police any more. She didn't trust him. She'd hardly acknowledged him since he'd left to be an actor. She'd never been entirely well. Her imagination. And there he sat, a man into his thirties, alerted by a super, holding her hand on New Year's Eve, as she talked to him toward the end as if he were her father, reciting the Westminster Shorter Catechism back at him.

And now he stood here older than she'd ever

been, the only person who retained her. Or his pop. Gone now, and all those years they'd lived together, also. The entirety of it gone, all lost, buried under the uses he'd made of it in greasepaint.

The furnace going colder in the center of the widening night of all the nights of all his years.

"Poppa John."

The clarity of her shape, in yellow, was so impressed in him, and the yellow so reduced by the bleaching effect of alcohol, her reappearance didn't register as different at first, except for the suffusion of color in her face, and then he saw her arms straight out from her shoulders, tense and bare, and then the light and dainty diadem of fluff below her waist. She was naked.

There was a metallic cracking at the door and a woman who looked his height, with blackish hair over her shoulders and a carriage so erect she seemed to be leaning back from the vertical, walked in on them where they stood, unmoving from the dancer's impact, and swung in abrupt turns from one to the other, then again, as if to register this forever.

"Merry Christmas," the dancer said, and floated her arms like a conductor's to the miniature voices still ba-beeing.

"Merry Christmas, my butt," the other said. Her arms gripped two bulky sacks, which might account for the angle of her stance, but didn't appear to. Now she swung on him with the entire force of her wide-set eyes, and beneath the heat of the affront in them, he saw a mist of inwardness he tried to relate to a memory of eyes on him like this before.

"You've been slop—" the dancer began. "I mean, shopping. You're half sloshed. Did you get something for me?"

"You're in rare shape yourself. I should have got you a raincoat."

"Oh, sape your shelf. I had two beers and a sip of his clear-plastic lightning. Hey!" She approached in springing steps in his periphery, while he kept his eyes on the other, as if to wrest the memory from her, and felt those hands enwrap his arm. "You haven't noticed. Here's Poppa John!"

"Why, you little slut," the other said, and slammed the bags down on the tiny table, setting it wobbling. "You always get what you want, don't you?"

"Hey, I brought him up to meet you. He's on a downer, though, I think, poor guy."

"Poppa John!" the other cried. "My God, it is you!"

She was to him in a rush and had her arms around him, not quite his height, and then kissed him on the mouth, a pillowy occlusion, and drew back, her hands still at his neck. She was the sort who set the original creature in him purring merely to be in her sight. She wouldn't let him look into her eyes now. She turned his aside at each attempt, and then the fringe of her lashes lowered as if to say *No*. Her nose was a sonorous line, like Isadora's, but abraded red at the nostrils, and her upper lip, lifting above her teeth in its fullness, was so plump its underside was fleshily wrinkled.

"How did you get here?" she asked.

"I met him in the street," the dancer said. "Or store, actually. We had a drink and I asked him up."

"Oh."

"To meet you."

"She did," he said, and felt the slush of liquor over his semi-rooted tongue. She released him.

"I was trying to blow *up!*"—imitating the voices—"whatever's got him so down."

"Between your big toes?" the other asked.

"Oh, please." The dancer stepped back, dipped, and did a sudden backflip, perfect.

The other took out a handkerchief and blew and rubbed her nose and wiped at what looked like tears.

"Who are you?" Poppa John asked.

Her stare went through this persiflage, past his feelings, to the area in him that had felt like an interior leaking, now a bleeding. "Deanne."

"Marsha!" the dancer said. "Now you say 'Poppa John,' Poppa John, and we'll all sing the Mickey Mouse Club song. '*Join* the tal-ent *round-up!*'" She went into a continuous cartwheel, spokes revolving without a rim into a blurred study only Leonardo might attempt, and then in a leap struck the trampoline, and came flipping over backward with a knee up, landing on pointed feet, as if on a stalk, with a soft thud that hardly shook her flesh.

"Would you cut the fritillary horseshit, Marsha!"

"Deanne," he said, "you are a wordsmith."

"I should hope," she said. "I'm supposed to be a writer." Her dark look issued up challenges.

"A writer."

"I write trash for a show like you used to be on. Well, not as good." She blew her nose again.

"The competition."

"Everybody steals from everybody else and they all come out about the same. Isn't that right?"

"Frocking A, Deanne." He couldn't quite say it.

"Poppa John!" she said.

"You think I'm that old coot you used to see on the tube?"

"Way to *go*, Poppa John!" the dancer cried.

"Oh, shut up," the other said. "Let's get out of here before she sits on you."

"Hey, don't take him away!"

"Get dressed, then," the other said, "and maybe you can come, too, sweetie."

"Sardines!" the dancer cried. She puckered her mouth, made popeyes, raised her hands up over her head, and rippled like a fish. "Sardines!"

"You know," the other said, "you're generally

a pretty nice person, which Poppa John probably hasn't had a chance to realize, except when you get like this, and then—it's mostly your mind, Marsha—you stink."

"Deanne," he said. "Goodness. Your friend here—"

"It's this job I'm up to my elbows in, she knows that. Come on, let's go."

"This began with her thinking of you, and—" He turned to confirm this, and discovered the dancer at his side, holding out the bag and smiling her widest smile.

Then her mouth silently formed the words *I love you.*

This bar was on Bleecker. From inside its murkiness, a long narrow window, beside a flight of steps he'd stumbled down, looked out at sidewalk level on a scene that seemed projected. Insubstantial legs moved as if in the missing half of the procession he'd watched outside the restaurant, scissoring the sun, which came in low from the west and appeared to lie in a solidified lance under his vision: the rail he put his foot on. An elbow over the bar held him firm. Great patterns of imagery, wound with words, would form at the front of his mind, about to break into landslides, and then topple backward into oblivion.

There were gaps of blackness between clear flashes he wasn't sure he hadn't imagined, when snapped back into acuity, especially in relation to her and her features, or the way their personalities would converge and run. The roots were extending out of his tailbone into the stool, sending tentacles deep, and the more rooted he became, the more he wanted to drink. He stared down, in a youthful blaze of nearsightedness alcohol could bring, at the striated cubes of the vodka he presently placidly sipped.

She was saying, "No, I was thinking of pushing for a young ex-minister, the liberal, loving, Lutheran sort, to work into the kind of position on our show you had on yours. But with more churchy authority. Maybe a minister still, but with wife problems. I mean, don't you think everybody steals from everybody else?"

"I suspect I haven't had the perspective, these last years, to see exactly what I was involved in, as I was doing it, with the discernment of an outside eye."

"All right. Pardon me. I'm sorry. You must have written your own stuff." She blew her nose and her features ran. "Did you?"

"I'd say about seventy-thirty."

"You?"

"The thirty, in recent years. The other way around before that. I had writers who came to understand what I was up to. I got special treatment. Do any on yours?"

"Oh, maybe two, at the most. But they're social content. One case of pure longevity."

"I'm grateful I was built up over the years with the care a couple of fellows took."

"Now, that sounds like the real Poppa John."

He'd seen the dancer revolving in the air in the way that the sun moved in the depths of this one's eyes inches away. "Do you think she might come?"

"She probably—" The eyes went on an inward search and came up thinking better of this. "I doubt it. All she's interested in is dancing and herself."

"She seemed so in you."

"Well, that."

"And can't find a job."

"It's difficult."

"But not for you."

"Oh, well, I've prostituted myself. All of Iowa is soap opera. I simply report on that. No, it's not, really. It's the same as here but under proper covers. Or kept under the skin. Contained. Things happen slower there and aren't as eruptive."

"So you support her?"

"Who?"

"Marsha. If that's her name."

"Sort of. She's had well-paying parts now and then. She's good. She works at it. She'll take menial jobs that'd drive me bonkers if there's a need for her to. She's O.K."

"You went to high school with her?"

She looked up and her eyes went parting into several sets. "We met at college. Why?"

"Identical accents."

"We're not gay."

"I didn't say that."

"All right, then I'll say this: I love her. She probably had to steel herself to do that. She's afraid to let most men see her one on one. She freezes up."

"So you see how I mean it. Certainly not in the way that you've loved the same wife."

"There was never a wife on—"

"I mean your *wife*. She obviously fills in all the empty spaces I can see in you right now—you're a mess—or you couldn't function or get from one day to the next, much less be a great actor. You should be with her now."

He stood, too rooted to move farther, though his bladder felt like a swelling melon belted with metal. To cover the pain and possible recourse, he said, "So it won't be the dark lady in this version."

"I don't get it."

"Shakespeare's sonnets. Or perhaps more fitting,

'In the twilight, in the evening, in the black and dark night.' " Then it came spurting out.

"You bastard," she said.

"You know Proverbs 7."

"You bet. My dad's an elder. He hit me with that when I left."

"I said it *won't*."

"As if you had any say."

Meanwhile, the burst like flame below his waist had eased, and was now a heated weight in his trousers, going in warm lengths down his legs and ankles, deflating his abdomen by degrees; and as it continued to come he watched it puddle wide from the sun-glazed width of dusty tile that held the window's shape, and dart in snaking trails of blackish shine toward the door.

"Poppa John!" she cried.

"Like icicles in June, my dear," he said, and shook his leg, which his trousers clung to as if stuck with blood.

The bartender, who was at the window, said, "Hey, what the!" in one of those loud unmusical voices, like the toneless blatting of a bad car horn, four levels over normal, that set Poppa John's nerves on edge. The man came and bent under the bar in front of them, saying into its cave, "It can't be that cooler any more, or this damn keg hookup, or better not be, Salomini Brothers Refrigeration, you jerks." Then he stood and did a little leap to lie on the bar and gripped its edge and looked down. He turned to Poppa John.

"Oh, for Christ's sake!" he cried in the blatting voice. "Go on, get out of here! I can't stand guys like you!"

"Oh, please," she said. "Take it easy. Give me a mop." She took Poppa John and led him to a table and chairs and sat him down—"No!" the man cried, "Out!"—and went back to the bar. "Hey, calm down and give me a mop. I'll make this right by you. He's not well."

"Yeah, sure, I know the kind. So old they can't control their bladders, and then they come in here with some young chick and stand at my bar and piss their ever-loving *pants!* I'm through with you both! I've had it!"

"How do you know he's not my dad?"

"Dad, schmad, I've seen you in here, too, snookums. All right!" He stomped down the clattery boards behind the bar toward its open end and Poppa John stood, draining again at the prospect of something physical, and saw the man grab up a mop in the corner and heave it like a javelin. Its head hit with a plop and thrashing of cords over his bubbling sneakers. "All right, then, *lady,* clean up after your beau! Me, I don't want to get in smelling distance of the crippled mess."

✳

The cold light of the snow-scoured air outside showed her skin to be flawless, the first he'd noticed; one of her nostrils was running toward the curve of her fleshy lip, and her eyes strained at him from out of surrounding red, furious inhabitants of endless fields and open space. "I've always wanted to meet you, to find out what goes on in your head, and what you're actually up to, and if this is what you're up to, it sucks."

"You must write searing dialogue."

"It sucks."

"Though repetitive in the manner of Heming—"

"You know, I used to think everything my folks said was platitudinous mush. *Monosyllabic* mush. God. God. God. But, buddy, they at least tried to live by what they said!"

She pulled down her lips with her fingers and his left ear rang with echoes at the piercing force of her whistle. Then his teeth started to chatter at the whistle's tuning to the understructure tightening from his shoes to his crotch.

"I'm getting you a cab. You go straight home."

"I never claimed to be anybody I acted."

"That wasn't acting!" Her eyes issued up the challenges again. "Then, when you were on that show, or now. I take everything everybody says at face value, no matter how it's said or what front it comes out of. It's the only way to live. After about a

year here, I learned that. And after a year here, everything my folks said proved true. Sure I'm an idealist,
and you became the only person I had to relate to.
Damn!"

"But you can't take a character I was and—"

"Oh, shut up. You're drunk. You talk too much.
If men like you get like this, what's the use. Who is
there to look up to?"

There was a slushy sound of slowing tires close,
then a cab's brakes, and it was as if he himself had
stopped: the shapes of the street asserted themselves
in solid hues. Then again his vision was affected by
the flickering animation, and cars and people passed
with the pause and then rush and pause of unreeling
on film.

"Don't stop anywhere," she said, and slipped the
strings of the bag into his hand. "Don't have another."

A door popped open behind, as if onto the city
and his place in it, and he piled in, half flailing, backward, feeling her hand in an armpit. He pulled in
his legs and flopped the bag over on the seat beside
him. "Oh," he said. He did his wave in the speeded-
up time of a silent. "Merry Christmas!"

She slammed the door and tossed back her hair,
also suddenly movielike, like all he now saw out the
window, and then drew up into her erect lean, and at
last smiled. The beauty of it was enough—

"Where to, friend?" the cabby asked.

—enough that a man of his age might hold on to it till death. "First, up to the corner." Which looked like part of a set of a small town he'd once worked on. "Go north a block there, turn left."

The meter clacked on and they whirred off into the traffic to its tick. "Then?"

Then he realized he wasn't sure he had the fare for an uptown trip. He wasn't about to look, with the man's eyes in the mirror on him. "My daughter and I have had a little disagreement." He craned around and saw her out the rear window, within its rocking frame, striding up the street in their direction, but with steps that appeared to propel her backward, for she continued to diminish, her head down and her hands in her pockets, her long black hair bannering back from her face and lashing in the seaside twilight that only these Village streets still seemed to contain, already immersed in herself and her style, with all of its murderous turns toward self-righteousness. *Just like me,* his conscience mocked.

"Let me out the first chance you get."

"Aw, hell," the cabby said, and slapped down the flag. "It's craziness, this goyisher holiday, pure craziness. You never know what's next." He dipped to a halt at the curb and Poppa John dug and discovered enough change. He pulled himself forward to pay and struck clear plastic and sat back. Some sort of lever led along the side of the cab to his door handle.

"When it gets to be Christmas," the man said, and turned to him, and Poppa John saw that the fellow was nearly his age, grizzled with grayish stubble, "a guy should just put away his change box and hang up the jock."

He went into the first bar he came to, wearing his real face, and thought, Cruel. Her. Her way of— His consciousness felt suspended from a fraying thread he had to move right not to snap. And move his thoughts in a careful crawl across. He ordered another of the same. The last of his cash. A handful of tokens. In a gathering grayness (he could hear the man at the other place blatting "Cheap-ass!") he tossed the tokens down as a tip.

Walk. He'd walk. He had to meet her at the bank.

Was that it?

He wasn't sure how he'd made it. It must be almost eight. He was afraid to look at his watch; it no longer made sense and its hands seemed to shift under the pressure of his need to figure them out. The cardboard ornament above, with its twining of tinsel, blocked and halved the purplish lamplight coming down in foggy beams, and appeared to draw closer to him with every breath he took. His trousers were stiff as leggings, he was numb across his privates and toes, and suffering chills and surges of panic and grief, along with a sensation that he was growing.

Snow was coming down again in gray and sleety bits, and in the darkness of the street its fall confused his placement. He seemed to lift. He could barely feel his hands, but sensed that ice was cracking away over their backs as they increased in size. He rubbed and slapped at them, the bag banging over his knees, and the sensation spread. He puffed, out of breath, fighting this, and the bulging clouds across his eyes drew him up higher. He checked the height of people passing, to assure himself that he was wrong, and his body responded with jerks worse than the chills.

A gangly man in a battered hat, with long blond hair sticking out of it, who looked like the actor cast as Ferdinand to his Prospero in '32, came along in furious strides, and then swung over to him as if in recognition, revealing a cut across his nose and spittle at the corners of his mouth, and thrust up his face, youngish, in its twenties, and cried, "Bark! Bark!"

A worm, less than a dog, came to Poppa John on the reek of the fellow's digested wine, and he went back as if struck. And though he braced himself, seemed to continue back into the place he'd been struggling to keep out of. He was his real size, or reduced, and the air blacker blue. Then there was a pressure on him from behind, as if Celia were inside after all, waiting. He went in. The organist smiled and continued to play "Joy to the World," as if resuming it from the first time he'd passed him.

Poppa John passed him, removing his beret, and the articulated diction of the chords, joined by the ringing of the carillon, penetrated him as if he were vapor. He saw worn and ragged sneakers moving over the stones of the floor below like somebody else's. Then dead silence. Barefoot like this across the stones of a temple courtyard. Palms out beyond the columns in a desert vista.

Then there was a tripping rupture of the remnants of sense that had held him aligned to reason just seconds before, and sound everywhere broke through. From the pealing coffers of the lit and vaulted ceiling, Celia's face traveled down at him on wires of flight, fragile and luminous in the cloche, and whispered into his ear, "Fifty cents."

And in a burst of whiteness was gone. He tasted crackers and milk. Chewed aspirin. His head was the place's interior and his limbs as weighty as the marble bench he lowered himself on. Again he saw the sneakers, and was startled by the verse, *How beautiful the feet of them that preach the gospel of peace.* And then, closing in on the other side, *For where your treasure is, there will your heart be also.*

No! Not to be flung, a disappearing dot, into infinite space! Vaporous sensations, the worst and best, freed from the authority of the mind—spittle and nose. This shaking knee the nape of a neck. A scream of his mother's over a toenail. *Celia!*

"*What is it, Poppa John?*"

And the moment when they'd been standing outside went ticking up to its beginning, to the lost and weighty thought her question had sealed, which dropped into him now in all its substantiality: *All there is to do is give up and admit you're not free.*

A stream of images went pouring from his eyes in the scalelike falling he'd read about but never been through, in flashing increments all the way back to his birth, and he thought: It's this? This simple? Simple? As simple as the music. Which affected him, he now knew, by embodying his feelings in forms that only an incarnation could be the original for and give substance to. Down in a body like this.

He felt the suffocating crush of his father's rough beard, and put up a hand to feel his own. "I've left," a voice like his father's said.

And then the curtain of his tabernacle ripped, the pole toppled, and the tent came down in tearing shreds.

Then a new and separate force approached in a rush, as down the open empty hall where his pop had disappeared so many nights, blowing open all the doors of all his senses to the frozen note where time revolved and wheeled: the presence of the man of sorrows, acquainted with his grief, Christ as Lord.

"Ah, God!" he cried. He was spared any sight, but in the terror of such perfection was a wormy slab of meat, rotten to the core, cancer-shot. Then a bloody redness bounded him in, and the face from the basement came sailing up at him in full release, free of the tilted perspective it always assumed, and he saw his father at last as he'd looked when he was alive, and then the face flew on out the back of his skull, and in its fracturing aftermath he was staring at a pair of bare feet, tensed in their final tremors, crossed at the arches, twitching and tearing over an iron spike.

To ever have held up his head in the light of this was monstrosity. Unspeakable presump—

The wind emptied out his ears.

He coughed and choked at the insurrection in him, while a younger man, deeper inside, patient and accomplished, trained to work at every hour, rose from another bench in the echoing darkness and sighed. It wasn't a bench. It was his cot. Ned at eleven. He started coming forward out of the basement.

Poppa John stood up. He was standing in the glacial moment that had supported him until now. He dropped the gifts and everything stilled in the ringing recollection of silence after a revolver's stomp. Only a faint noise as of a distant jet towing the last of his thoughts out over the sea, while his heart held here.

He went to the window and with the help of the scooped ledge below its bars lowered himself to his knees. "Forgive me, Father," he whispered, in a harsh feat of speech. "I have sinned. It's been sixty years since— Ah, God, *please!* This is worse than eternity!"

Then he is back on the bench before he's begun, interrupted by the old priest. "What the hell!" Ricocheting voice. Others hiss by. One turns from their sideboard. No, bars. Is this Celia's bench? These heated creatures crowding around, arms over him, and such a clattering of heels and shoes it seems the hooves below have started to dance. The old gray guard, not priest, beside him in a trembling hug.

"Get back. All out. Closing. We're closed."

The old guard up now, now walks off to shoo, now has a limp, preacher grandfather the size of Ned, the two reversed, and saws or taps and saws over his uniform with flying hands to his side, his holster, to unpack for the *coup de grâce*, this last twittering cell of fading consciousness left, but has a dustrag, a huge handkerchief, waving instead. "Oh, goodness," he says, and smothers his face and fires off a report. "Goodness, God, it's Poppa John."

And is back beside him, on the same side, holding him in the trembling hug.

Then thighs of blue come down on the other,

peppered with drips and speckles of black. The police. Open overcoat and polish of leather, plus the pistol Poppa John tries to get at. "Hey! Easy, old fella. I mean, Poppa John."

One frisks him and there's a cold square over his heart where his wallet was, while he rocks to find the rhythm that will free him from this for good.

"Yes, somebody call, please." The police.

"Hurry! He's low." The guard.

Was that it?

Blankness. And then, as he leans toward the badge and chest, into the arms of blue, oblivion.

Then Celia is there, in front of him, holding his hands, which swell with stitching heat. The rest go off. "Let her see."

There's something wrong around her face or head, and her expression, her eyes. She whispers, "How many times have you said this would never happen again, Poppa John? How could you, on this day of all days, when—"

He is so stunned by this, his foot stabs to make him stay.

"See? You're three sheets to the wind. Oh, please, whatever happens, however bad it gets, don't turn into one of those brothers I had to play nursemaid for."

Poppa John

All of this enters in a pouring stream, as absolute as lava, and then she looks in and sees him looking out from his den of utter defenselessness.

Then all there is is the shape of her retreating back as she walks away alone across the vaulted space.

SUNDAY /

P_{oppa} John slept on.

When he'd awakened the first time, he wanted to know if his gifts had got to Celia. They had, he was told. He was aware that he was alive but was so obviously at the verge of the opposite that he wanted matters in order.

He slept on.

Then, in this or in waking, there was a man or a woman outside his door, or a man and woman were there, leaning over a slab where chessmen stood, and beyond them, against a background of blue, another group was moving in response to their moves on the board. His position in the pattern they were moving toward was the square of the bed he lay upon. Branches of a tree nodded outside the other wall, which was a window. There was snow or sleet covering the tree. All icy. This was a hospital.

After the echo of Celia's walk, she and the policeman got him into a cab and got him here, and he had to wait in a room that was bare except for a row of booths along one wall, like carrels off a gallery, separated from her, as if all reality had taken on the aspect of dreams. There was a form to sign which said he would commit himself. It had to be explained to him. She was talking to the director, he was told, and wouldn't be allowed to see him, anyway, until after he saw his psychiatrist.

And then the man was there in a rush, in a Russian fur hat and greatcoat, or Russian in its voluminousness, aromatic of winter, and pulled up a chair so near that his knees nudged Poppa John's. The man shrugged the fur, and stared straight into his defenselessness.

"Can you tell me how you feel, Ned?"

The man needed a shave, harrowing, since his whiskers were now gray, and a hand went there as if to acknowledge this. "Ned, can you talk to me?"

"Haven't I tried?"

"It's that bad, huh?"

"Worse."

"Why did you let it go so long?"

Silence.

"Try to make yourself talk. That might help."

"I couldn't pay you." He was eleven again.

"We would have worked that out. This is going to end up costing you more."

"Then it wouldn't have happened. I'm glad it did."

"Can you tell me about that?"

"Can I?"

"You're tired, Ned."

"Yes, I am."

"Why don't we get you on some medication and get you to bed." In pulling out his pad, he saw. "Oh. What happened to your trousers?"

"I wet them."

"Goodness, it came down that hard, huh?" His eyes lunged.

"This was earlier."

Poppa John felt taken care of, doctored, and about to fall asleep.

"You know, from what I'd gathered, I mean, from what Celia said when she called, you're not as crazy as I expected."

And when he woke in the square of the bed, in the pattern moving toward him, covered by sunlight from the window at his feet, a sheet lay over him with the folds it had had when he'd died as Poppa John. But now its fabric was of a cellular mesh he could see through to his own cells, and it spread and touched the walls with living seams. He plucked at it, and white-tinted shadow billowed the air, which was composed of particles as white as the fabric itself. He raised up and realized how his grandfather had pulled a last sheet over himself like this, as his father had lifted his last one away on that last morning. And was released into their lives.

Or what he carried of them was leaving, for he lay down again in sleep.

He slept on.

Drawing into narrowing depths the branches outside, which held snow along their lengths and formed, against a square like a page, a calligraphy that came to spell (once the language was discerned) GREEN.

There was the *puhsh puhsh* pu-*ish* of something being inflated next to his ear, and his upper arm floated in a surrounding squeeze. A mustached man in white listened through tubes until the arm went down with a hiss. This must be the one who'd brought him a pair of pills and a paper cup his first night, and then asked him to hurry up, as he'd sat on the bed in his suit and topcoat, so they could take his temperature, rectally, the fellow said, because of the cold water for the pills, and get him to bed. The gulp of the pills caught on a sob, since he knew he'd end up like them, two little turds, which the black maid with her mop would swab up in the morning.

Then the liquid stick of cold intrusion.

Now the fellow said, "You damn near could have died of a heart attack on top of it all, and now you've got pneumonia, Pops." And then licked a thumb and turned over pages on an aluminum clipboard.

"Brud pressure's *row*," Poppa John said, as if to reassure the man, and was alarmed at how his vocal apparatus, his life, had been affected by the pills after all.

"Tell me about it, baby," the man said.

And then to wake to his feet being rubbed and to see, against the projected grain of movielike light from the window, the dazzling woman who'd brought the parcel to their flat that day, bending to minister to him. It's Celia. There are paths like maplike portions of the morning light of their apartment over her face.

"I'm here," she says.

"Yes."

"Forgive me, please. I thought—"

He nods; she means seeing him in the bank.

"You've been true to character," she says.

"What?"

"Holding out like this. Like not asking for a meal when it was the one thing you needed most. How I love you."

He slips into sleep and his sleep goes on.

Bright morning of another time. The psychiatrist came up the hall, came past his room, struck by the light, and was gone. He lay waiting, in the throes of a squirm (from the medication?) that wouldn't allow him to keep his sheet and boundaries quelled, checking that slippery watch and sipping water to loosen his tongue. The psychiatrist was at the door. He held the aluminum clipboard against his stomach and noted something on it in a miniature hand that tensed his face. A suit and tie. He let his arms fall and stepped to the perimeter of a giving seam.

"Hi, Ned." How quiet. "Do you know what day it is?"

"No."

"Should I tell you?"

"Why not?"

"Sure, why not? People pay me to tell them what to do, so why not tell you the day, huh? Remember it, though, in case somebody comes in in a while and asks. It'll be a point for you. It's Sunday."

"Oh."

"It's Christmas. Shouldn't I see you on Sunday?" He smiled, and his jowly face achieved a greater breadth.

"Acts of necessity and mercy."

"But if I kept that set of rules, if I was rigid about them, would I always know what was what?"

"They're rules, yes, with nothing behind them."

"Did you get stuck on them, Ned?"

"Yes, I did."

"You know, you give me insight."

"Oh."

"In the way that you can dispense such wonderful advice, *a-heh heh*, and hardly see your own hand."

"How true."

"Are you crazier than two days ago?"

"That's your business."

The man glanced around at the whiteness, and then at the door, then back, and whispered, "Some here question my approach, I've heard, so you might be less crazy to them than I am. This is a relativistic business."

"I concede."

"You know——" He stepped one step farther, as if to see into the center of the man in the square, treading lightly for his size, cautious, and pursed his lips for the import of this. "You know, I *like* you. I'm really pleased you seem so well."

"Well, the pneumonia." Poppa John glanced at his wrinkled hands, liver-spotted over their backs, and remembered the girl saying he was her dad. Did her fingers curl up like this, or the other's?

"Listen. Nine out of ten patients who end up here have something physically wrong with them. It doesn't show up just in your head. It's not as simple as we'd like."

"I'm not ashamed of— I mean, I'm ashamed about the people who had nothing to do with it, and were bystanders, if they were affected, but not the impulse."

"Good."

"I might not need you."

"Well—" The man's eyes narrowed and made a series of interior calculations. "Let's put that possibility aside for now. I mean, since you're here. It's up to me to release you, you know. But let's assume I could make the same sort of living without your visits, and not be so concerned, considering the way things are working out for you."

"Good for you."

"Your progress has been amazing—"

"Grace."

"You know, I'm going to put something in my report about your spirit." He had a finger raised, shaking, as if to remember this, and now raised the clipboard and put his pen to it.

"Spirit it is." This was a whisper.

The man looked out the window, as if thinking of something else. "But I think we— I think both of us should have a look at some of the things that led to this. You're way on in years, Poppa John, to be having a breakdown."

"Breakdown?"

"How would you describe it?"

Silence.

"I was broken down." Silence. "I'll look at it. But the way that I see it might seem to you reversed."

"How's that?"

"I'm afraid you'll laugh if I say it."

"Give me a try."

"I believe in God."

"Well, you know, coming from you, that *is* tough to take. With a straight face, I mean. I mean, considering how I know you and your *image*. But don't feel bad." He faked some furtive glances around the room and brought his face, its jowls aquiver, within smelling range of his after shave, something musk, as his eyes widened. "Sometimes I do, too."

He drew back, and the teacher stepped into him, ready to give himself for a student. "Or, actually, most of us do, at one time or another. When we're trapped, or in trouble or danger, and there's no way out. Or if you're sure you're going to catch it for something you just did. Or you're at a beach, say, and in the right mood just as you look out over the ocean, and suddenly it's all opened up to you."

His hands, with the glinting clipboard in one, swung wide to illustrate this, and the metal sent a burst of cymbaling light through the room.

"I should say, 'Christ,'" Poppa John said, subdued.

"Well, in that respect, let me put it this way: I don't agree with all of that, I'm sure, but don't think it's my perogative to say it couldn't be right for you. I don't believe I should limit spiritual impulses—the creative in you—any more than I'd limit others that might be leading in the direction that could heal you. We're each that different, *Poppa John*. If this particular flower is starting to blossom along those lines at last, like one of those century plants I have, and is behind the face, or is the face, masked, then we should see if we can't coax it into completeness, on its own terms. Wouldn't that be nice?"

His partial smile, with his lips parted, conveyed kindness, and was an alert to a leaping application of humor; and then he said, "Now, why'd you piss your pants?"

His laughter began at his stomach, building, while he kept his eyes on Poppa John's as he laughed, and then the "transfer" that Poppa John had read about, and had sensed with the man before, became a complete exchange, and Poppa John lifted a hand to say how he loved this man for helping him over the years as he had.

"Wait till I shrink you," the man said, and then saw the change, and stepped and put a hand on Poppa John's arm, then on the bed. "Depressed?"

Poppa John shook his head.

"Meanwhile, I'll tell Celia to come in."

"Celia's here?"

"Waiting. You can have the day with her between injections."

"Injections?"

"I'm going to fix up the pneumonia in that lung. That's where we shrinks have it over psychologists, or counselors, or dabblers in the Gestalt— Need I mention priests?"

"I have a heavenly."

"Anyway, that's why we shrinks are so great. We're *medical* doctors. Check the parable of the Good Samaritan again. Luke, ah—" He pointed a finger at his temple and closed his eyes, a suicidal pose, exposing his lower teeth, and said, "Luke, ah, 10."

Then he went out with his lower lip between his teeth, writing below his chest in his miniature hand as he walked.

She was in the rust-colored suit and brown sweater and black hat, and the makeup around her eyes looked darker but more artfully applied. She kissed him and then turned in the light, exposing a blue-gray eye to a chasm of sun, and then revolved several times, as she did for him when he'd buttoned her up or she'd walked in in a new outfit, transporting him back to his blue chair, with the walls of books around, and as she paused in her revolutions (revealing the miniature shopping bag under a new black coat draped over an arm) there was a catch at his attention. "What do you think?" she asked.

"Sell the television," he said.

"What?"

"Sell it. I want the years left to be full and our own."

"Fine. We can use the income." She dropped her things in a chair and pulled at the cuffs of the suit as if she'd just fitted herself into it. "Well, what do you think? Do you like it?"

"I guess."

"I took everything home and opened it the same night. I'm sorry. I couldn't help it. It was my solace, if such can be called that."

"I didn't expect you to wait."

"I expected more than 'I guess,' I guess. Though I don't know the history. It seems more appropriate for a woman a few decades younger." She removed the hat and shook out her hair, which had been cut short. It was the difference he'd seen at the bank.

"Oh!" he said, and saw the girl catapulting up into the air above her trampoline.

"I feel like a Village vamp in it."

"Oh."

"But if it's what you want me to wear, wear it I shall."

"Good." Which came down with the thump of her feet on the floor. Over.

"I've decided not to ask you what you were up to that entire day. At least not for a while."

"I'll tell you."

"No, not on Christmas. Here." She pulled a package out of the shopping bag and laid it over his stomach. He was psychic, usually, about her gifts to him, but in his condition the ballast of this didn't correspond to its size, which was about the size of a shirt box.

She pulled up a chair by its chromium arms and sat in it as he picked at the wrappings with medication-weakened fingers, seeing his grandfather's fingers, turned up at the tips like this, tremble beneath his; his difficulty with tasks like unwrapping.

"Aren't you going to guess?" she asked.

"A leather shirt."

"Oh, *damn*."

"Is it?"

"Open it!"

The box read *Crouch & Fitzgerald* in one corner, and he could picture the wide window he sometimes paused along, on rounds, checking his reflection among the displays, while he thought of the times he'd traveled when he was young, and often wished he still did, partly as an excuse to indulge himself here: the bitter smell of leather from the door affirmed the force of this desire, and was rising from the box now. He took off its top and lifted away the tissue and saw a shining brown portfolio, with a brass clasp at the lip of its fold-over flap, and gold-stamped initials below. *N.E.D.*

He ran his fingers over the inset of them as if blinded by the way they italicized and shuffled and transposed in a light like the light from the furnace room.

She was standing beside him. "Do the initials upset you? It's your name."

"Oh, no, wonderful. It isn't that. No."

"What?"

"Your confidence."

"What do you mean?"

"That I'll have a career, still, to use it for."

"Oh, of course you will. I thought you should work up more of your background, rather than sailing along on reputation, and carry it with you. There's something inside."

He worked the button of the clasp and folded back the flap and took out an envelope addressed: "To N.E.D. who was Ned to me before Poppa John and is Ned to me now."

Inside was a card that said only *You* on its front and inside . . . *are the one,* along with something that fluttered over his chest. It was a cashier's check drawn on their bank for two hundred dollars.

"Where did you get this?"

"You gave me so much, and I had a little saved somewhere else than in that jewelry box we both kept stealing from. I thought if you didn't have to worry about the rent for a month, you could keep your eyes ahead."

"What about paying for this place?"

"You could get help at your age. Also, I think you should shave off your beard."

"Oh."

"I'd love to see your face again." She put a hand on his cheek. "How do you feel, dear, really."

"On a plateau, in an enormous room."

"At least it's not one that's been prepared for you."

"They all are, in a sense. But more as in 'a large place.' That sense of it."

"Psalms."

He studied her now, and saw that she'd indeed refined her makeup to the newest look beginning to appear in the magazines. "How do you know that?"

"I'm able to read."

"You've been reading my Bible."

"I'm not sure it's yours. One of the many around, along with the library you've weaved through the apartment." She picked up the shopping bag and tipped it and slid his Thompson chain-reference over his stomach, returning those mornings when he'd awakened with the weight of it there. "Here's the one you used to use so much."

"How long?"

"What?"

"Have you been reading?"

"About a year." She looked as she had when she'd handed him her father's Shakespeare. "Every day since you died as Poppa John. Whenever you went off or I could be alone in my powder room. I believe I've believed since then. The way you carried off your death, and the way it affected me, and the work you went into to prepare for it, gave me an inkling of the reality of his, and all he must have gone through."

"Oh, my God."

"I've been waiting for you to suggest that we go to a church like one of the ones we first went to when you were so serious about your role. I've seen you fight this every step of the way and had to let you."

"Why didn't you say something?"

"It wasn't my place, is it, and can't one sanctify one's unbelieving husband?"

Again she smiled, with that endless blur of her feet coming down those stairs, never at rest in his interior, and he felt rivers of living feeling over his face.

"How I love you," he cried. "How I love him!"

"Your pop?"

"Oh, ah—" He had thought that his point of reference would be as particular to her as it was to him, and now realized that some of their own conversations, even, would be reversing beyond one another in their separate efforts to reach and please. "Yes," he said. "Well, yes," he said, and folded his hands over the sheet and saw the mountainous snows that would cover his grave. "Yes," he said. "And further afield."

"Pardon, Poppa John?"

"How true."

Printed in the USA
CPSIA information can be obtained
at www.ICGtesting.com
LVHW091133150724
785511LV00001B/110

9 780374 526733